Brander Matthews

With my Friends

Tales Told in Partnership

Brander Matthews

With my Friends
Tales Told in Partnership

ISBN/EAN: 9783337030308

Printed in Europe, USA, Canada, Australia, Japan

Cover: Foto ©Andreas Hilbeck / pixelio.de

More available books at **www.hansebooks.com**

WITH MY FRIENDS

BY THE SAME AUTHOR:

THE THEATRES OF PARIS.

FRENCH DRAMATISTS OF THE 19TH CENTURY.

A FAMILY TREE, AND OTHER STORIES.

THE LAST MEETING: A Story.

A SECRET OF THE SEA, AND OTHER STORIES.

PEN AND INK: Papers on Subjects of More or
Less Importance.

WITH MY FRIENDS

TALES TOLD IN PARTNERSHIP

BY

BRANDER MATTHEWS

WITH AN INTRODUCTORY ESSAY ON

The Art and Mystery of Collaboration

NEW YORK

LONGMANS, GREEN, & CO.

15 EAST SIXTEENTH STREET

1891

TO THE FRIENDS

WHO WROTE THESE STORIES WITH ME

I INSCRIBE THEM.

B. M.

New York, October, 1891.

CONTENTS

THE ART AND MYSTERY OF COLLABORATION.

IT may be said that curiosity is the only useful vice, since without it there would be neither dis· covery nor invention; and curiosity it is which lends interest to many a book written in collaboration, the reader being less concerned about the merits of the work than he is with guessing at the respective shares of the associated authors. To many of us a novel by two writers is merely a puzzle, and we seek to solve the enigma of its double authorship, accepting it as a nut to crack even when the kernel is little likely to be more digestible than the shell. Before a play of Beaumont and Fletcher or a novel of MM. Erckmann-Chatrian not a few find themselves asking a double question. First, " what was the part of each partner in the writing of the book ? " And, second, " how is it possible for two men to be concerned in the making of one work ? "

The answer to the first question can hardly ever be given; even the collaborators themselves are at

a loss to specify their own contributions. When
two men have worked together honestly and heartily in the inventing, the developing, the construct-
ing, the writing, and the revising of a book or a
play, it is often impossible for either partner to pick
out his own share; certain things he may recognize
as his own, and certain other things he may credit
frankly to his ally; but the rest was the result of
the collaboration itself, contributed by both parties
together and not by either separately. To explain
this more in detail calls for an answer to the second
question, and requires a careful consideration of the
principle of collaboration, and a tentative explanation of the manner in which two men may write one
book.

I confine myself to a discussion of literary partnerships, because in literature collaboration is more
complete, more intimate than it is in the other arts.
When an architect aids a sculptor, when Mr. Stam-
ford White, for instance, plans the mounting of the
'Lincoln' or the 'Farragut' of Mr. Saint Gaudens,
the respective shares of each artist may be determined with precision. So it is also when we find
Rubens painting the figures in a landscape of Sny-
ders. Nor are we under any doubt as to the contribution of each collaborator when we hear an

operetta by Mr. Gilbert and Sir Arthur Sullivan;
we know that one wrote the words and the other
the music, and the division of labor does not seem
unnatural, although it is not necessary; Wagner, for
example, composed the score to his own book. But
no one is puzzled by the White-Saint Gaudens combination, the Rubens-Snyders, or the Gilbert and
Sullivan, as most of us are, for example, by the alli-
ance of Charles Dickens and Wilkie Collins in the
writing of ' No Thoroughfare.'

If the doubt is great before a novellette composed by two authors of individualities as distinct
as those of Dickens and of Collins, how much greater
may it be before books written by more than two
partners. Not long ago, four clever American
story-tellers co-operated in writing a satirical tale,
' The King's Men;' and years before four brilliant
French writers, Mme. de Girardin, Gautier, Sandeau
and Méry, had set them the example by composing
that epistolary romance, 'La Croix de Berny.'
There is an English story in six chapters by six
authors, among whom were the younger Hood, the
late T. W. Robertson, and Mr. W. S. Gilbert; and
there is an American story happily entitled, ' Six
of One, by Half-a-dozen of the Other '—Mrs. Stowe
being among the half-dozen.

Six authors for a single story, or even four, may seem to some a woeful waste of effort, and so, no doubt, it is; but I have found recorded cases of more extravagant prodigality. In France, an association of three or four in the authorship of a farce is not at all uncommon; and it is there that collaboration has been carried to its most absurd extreme. M. Jules Goizet, in his curious 'Histoire Anecdotique de la Collaboration au Théâtre' (Paris, 1867), mentions a one-act play which was performed in Paris in 1811, and which was the work of twenty-four dramatists; and he records the production in 1834, and also in Paris, of another one-act play, which was prepared for a benefit of the Dramatic Authors' Society, and which had no fewer than thirty-six authors. This suggests an intellectual poverty as barren as that once satirized by Chamfort in Prussia, when, after he had said a good thing, he saw the others talking it over at the end of the table: " See those Germans," he cried, " clubbing together to take a joke."

For the most part these combination ventures are mere curiosities of literature. Nothing of real value is likely to be manufactured by a joint stock company of unlimited authorship. The literary partnerships whose paper sells on 'Change at par have

but two members.   It is this association of two, and
of two only, to which we refer generally when we
speak of collaboration.   In fact, literary collaboration might be defined, fairly enough, as "the union
of two writers for the production of one book."
This is, of a truth, the only collaboration worthy
of serious criticism, the only one really pregnant
and vital.

Like any other partnership, a collaboration is un-
satisfactory and unsuccessful unless it is founded on
mutual esteem.   The partners must have sympathy
for each other, and respect.   Each must be tolerant
of the other's opinions.   Each must be ready to
yield a point when need be.   In all associations
there must be concessions from one to the other.
These are the negative qualities of a good collaborator; and chief among the positive necessities is the
willingness of each to do his full share of the work.
A French wit has declared that the happiest marriages are those in which one is loved and the other
lets himself (or herself) be loved.   Collaboration is
a sort of marriage, but the witticism does not here
hold true, although Mr. Andrew Lang recently declared that in most collaborations one man did all
the work while the other man looked on.   No doubt
this happens now and again, but a partnership of

this kind is not likely to last long. Mr. Lang has also quoted from the 'Souvenirs Dramatiques' of the elder Dumas an opinion of that most delightful of romancers, to the effect that when two men are at work together "one is always the dupe, and *he* is the man of talent."

It is pleasant to be able to controvert the testimony of the great Dumas by the exhibits in his own case. Of all the mighty mass of Dumas's work, what survives now, a score of years after his death, and what bids fair to survive at least three score and ten years longer, are two or three cycles of brilliant and exciting narratives: 'Monte Cristo,' the 'Three Musketeers,' with its sequels, the stories of which Chicot is the hero; and of these every one was written in collaboration with M. Auguste Maquet.

Scribe is perhaps the only contemporary author who rivalled Dumas in fecundity and in popularity; and Scribe's evidence contradicts Dumas's, although both were persistent collaborators. Of all the hundred of Scribe's plays, scarce half a dozen were written by him unaided. When he collected his writings into a uniform edition, he dedicated this to his many collaborators; and he declared that while the few works he had composed alone were hard labor, those which he had done in partnership were a pleasure. And we know from M. Legouvé, one of Scribe's associates, that Scribe generally preferred to do all the mere writing himself. The late Eugène Labiche, almost as prolific a playwright as Scribe and quite as popular, did nothing except with a partner; and he, so we are told by M. Augier, who once composed a comedy with him, also liked to do all the actual writing.

In a genuine collaboration, when the joint work is a true chemical union and not a mere mechanical mixture, it matters little who holds the pen. The main advantage of a literary partnership is in the thorough discussion of the central idea and of its presentation in every possible aspect. Art and genius, so Voltaire asserted, consist in finding all that is in one's subject, and in not seeking outside of it. When a situation has been talked over thoroughly and traced out to its logical conclusion, and when a character has been considered from every angle and developed to its inevitable end, ninetenths of the task is accomplished. The putting down on paper of the situation and the character is but the clothing of a babe already alive and kicking.

Perhaps the unity of impression which we get from some books written in partnership is due to

the fact that the writing was always the work of
the same partner.   Scribe, for example, was not an
author of salient individuality, but the plays which
bear his name are unmistakably his handiwork.
Labiche also, like Scribe, was ready to collaborate
with anybody and everybody; but his trade-mark is
woven into the texture of every play that bears his
name.   It is understood that the tales of MM.
Erckmann-Chatrian are written out by M. Erckmann
and revised by M. Chatrian.   I have heard, on what
authority I cannot say, that of the long series of
stories bearing the names of Besant and Rice, all
that the late James Rice actually wrote with his own
pen was the first chapter or two of their first book,
'Ready Money Mortiboy.'   This assertion, whether
well founded or not, gains color of truth from the
striking similarity of style, not to call it identity, of
the Besant and Rice novels with the novels of the
surviving member of the partnership.   Yet, if one
may judge by the preface he has prefixed to the
library edition of 'Ready Money Mortiboy,' Mr.
Besant would be the last one to deny that Mr. Rice
was a full partner in the firm, bearing an equal share
in the burden and heat of the day.   Comparing the
novels of dual authorship with those of the survivor
alone, it is perhaps possible to ascribe to Mr. Rice

a fancy for foreign characters and a faculty of ren-
dering them vigorously, a curious scent for actual
oddity, a bolder handling than Mr. Besant's, and a
stronger fondness for dramatic incident, not to say
melodramatic. The joint novels have a certain kin-
ship to the virile tales of Charles Reade; but little
trace of this family likeness is to be found in the
later works of Mr. Besant alone, whose manner is
gentler and more caressing, with a more delicate
humor and a subtler flavor of irony.

But any endeavor to sift out the contribution of
one collaborator from that of his fellow is futile—if
the union has been a true marriage. It leads to the
splitting of hairs and to the building of more than
one hypothesis on the point of a single needle—
surely as idle a task as any ever attempted by a
Shakespearian commentator. I doubt, indeed, if this
effort "to go behind the returns"—to use an Americanism as expressive as an Americanism ought to
be—is even permissible, except possibly after the
partnership is dissolved. Under the most favorable
circumstances the inquiry is little likely to be profitable. Who shall declare whether the father or the
mother is the real parent of a child?

It is interesting, no doubt, and often instructive
to note the influence of two authors on each other;

to consider the effect of the combination of their
diverse talents and temperaments; to discover how
the genius of one conflicts with that of the other or
complements it; to observe how at one point the
strength of A reinforces the weakness of B, and how
at another point the finer taste of B adroitly curbs
the more exuberant energy of A; and to remark
how the conjunction of two men of like minds and
of equally ardent convictions sometimes will result
in a work harsher and more strenuous than either
would produce alone.

For curious investigation of this sort there is no
lack of material, since collaboration has been attractive to not a few of the foremost figures in the
history of literature.   The list includes not only
Beaumont and Fletcher among the mighty Eliza-
bethans, but Shakespeare and almost every one of
his fellow-dramatists—not only Corneille, Molière,
and Racine, but almost every other notable name
in the history of the French theatre.   Cervantes
and Calderon and Lope de Vega took partners in
Spain; and in Germany Schiller and Goethe worked
together.   In Great Britain Addison and Steele
united in the *Spectator*, and in the United States
Irving and Paulding combined in 'Salmagundi,' as
did Drake and Halleck in the 'Croakers.'

The list might be extended almost indefinitely, but it is long enough to allow of one observation—an observation sufficiently obvious. It is that no great poem has ever been written by two men together, nor any really great novel. Collaboration has served the cause of periodical literature. But it has been most frequent and most fertile among dramatists. We ask why this is—and the answer is ready. It is because a play calls primarily for forethought, ingenuity, construction, and compression, in the attaining of which two heads are indubitably better than one. And here we are nigh to laying hold on the root of the matter. Here we have ready to hand what may help towards a definition of the possibilities and of the limitations of literary partnership.

Collaboration fails to satisfy when there is need of profound meditation, of solemn self-interrogation, or of lofty imagination lifting itself freely towards the twin-peaks of Parnassus. Where there may be a joy in the power of unexpected expansion, and where there may be a charm of veiled beauty, vague and fleeting, visible at a glimpse only and intangible always, two men would be each in the other's way. In the effort to fix these fugitive graces they would but trip over each other's heels. A task of this delicacy belongs of right to the lonely student in the silent watches of the night, or in solitary walks under the greenwood tree and far from the madding crowd.

Collaboration succeeds most abundantly where clearness is needed, where precision, skill, and logic are looked for, where we expect simplicity of motive, sharpness of outline, ingenuity of construction, and cleverness of effect. Collaboration may be a potent coadjutor wherever technic is a pleasure for its own sake :—and the sense of art is dull in a time or in a place which does not delight in sound workmanship, and in the adroit devices of a loving craftsman. Perhaps, indeed, collaboration may tend—or, at least, it may be tempted now and again—to sacrifice matter to manner. Those enamored of technic may consider rather the excellence of the form than the value of the fact upon which their art is to be exercised. Yet it may be doubted whether there is any real danger to literature in a craving for the utmost technical skill.

In much of Byron's work Matthew Arnold found " neither deliberate scientific construction, nor yet the instinctive artistic creation of poetic wholes." Accidental excellence, an intuitive attaining of the ideal, the instinctive artistic creation of poetic

wholes, is not to be expected from a partnership—
indeed, is hardly possible to it. But a partnership
is likely to attempt deliberate scientific construction
owing to the mutual criticism of the joint authors;
and by collaboration the principles of scientific construction are conveyed from one to another to the
advancement of the art itself and to the unmistaka-
ble improvement of the mere journeyman work of
the average man of letters. For example, many
even of the best English novels seem formless when
compared with the masterly structure of any good
French story; and perhaps the habit of collaboration which obtains in France is partly to be praised
for this.

All things have the defect of their qualities as
well as the quality of their defects. Collaboration
may be considered as a labor-saving device; and,
like other labor-saving devices, it sometimes results
in a loss of individuality. One is inclined to suspect
a lack of spontaneity in the works which two authors
have written together, and in which we are likely to
find polish, finish, and perfection of mechanism.
To call the result of collaboration often over-labored,
or to condemn it as cut and dried, would be to ex-
press with unduly brutal frankness the criticism it
is best merely to suggest. By the very fact of a

partnership with its talking over, its searching discussion, its untiring pursuit of the idea into the most remote fastnesses, there may be an over-sharpness of outline, a deprivation of that vagueness of contour not seldom strangely fascinating.

No doubt in the work of two men there is a loss of the unexpected, and the story must of necessity move straight forward by the shortest road, not lingering by the wayside in hope of wind-falls. There is less chance of unforeseen developments suggesting themselves as the pen speeds on its way across the paper—and every writer knows how the pen often runs away with him "across country" and over many a five-barred gate which he had never intended to take: but as there is less chance of the unforeseen, so is there also less chance that the unforeseen will be worth having. Above all is there far less likelihood of the writer's suddenly finding himself up a blind-alley with a sign of No Thoroughfare staring him in the face. It has been objected that in books prepared in partnership even the writing is hard and arid, as though each writer were working on a foreign suggestion and lacking the freedom with which a man may treat his own invention. If a writer feels thus, the partnership is unprofitable and unnatural, and he had best get a divorce as soon as may be. In a genuine collaboration each of the parties thereto ought to have so far contributed to the story that he can consider every incident to be his, and his the whole work when it is completed.

As it happens there is one department of literature in which the defect of collaboration almost becomes a quality. For a drama deliberate scientific construction is absolutely essential. In play-making an author must know the last word before he sets down the first. From the rigid limitations of time and space there is no room on the stage for unexpected development. Voltaire tells us that there were misers before the invention of money; and no doubt there were literary partnerships before the first playhouse was built. But the value of collaboration to the playwright has been instinctively recognized whenever and wherever the theatre has flourished most abundantly; and as soon as the dramas of a country are of domestic manufacture, and cease to be mainly imported from abroad, the playmakers take to collaboration intuitively.

In Spain, when Lope de Vega and Calderon and Cervantes were writing for the stage, they had partners and pupils. In England there was scarce one of all the marvellous company of the Elizabethan dramatists who did not join hands in the making of plays. Fletcher, for example, wrote with Massinger even while Beaumont was alive. Chapman had for associates Marston, and Shirley, and Ben Jonson. Dekker worked in partnership with Ford, Webster, Massinger, and Middleton; while Middleton combined with Dekker, Fletcher, Rowley, and Ben Jonson.

In France, a country where the true principles of the play-maker's art are most thoroughly understood, Rotrou and Corneille worked together with three others on five-act tragedies barely outlined by Cardinal Richelieu. Corneille and Quinault aided Molière in the writing of 'Psyché.' Boileau and La Fontaine and other friends helped Racine to complete the 'Plaideurs.' In the present century, when the supremacy of the French drama is again indisputable, many of the best plays are due to collaboration. Scribe and M. Legouvé wrote together 'Adrienne Lecouvreur' and the 'Bataille des Dames.' MM. Meilhac and Halévy were joint authors of 'Frou-frou' (that poignant picture of the disadvantages of self-sacrifice) and of the 'Grand Duchess of Gerolstein' (that bold and brilliant satire of imperial misrule). Emile Augier, to my mind the most wholesome and the most manly dramatist of our day, joined Jules Sandeau in composing the 'Gendre de M. Poirier,' the strongest comedy of the century.

Scribe and Augier and Sandeau, M. Legouvé, M. Meilhac and M. Halévy, are all men of fine talents and of varied accomplishments in letters; they are individually the authors of many another drama; but no one of these other pieces attains the stature of the co-operative plays or even approaches the standard thus set. Nothing else of Scribe's is as human and as pathetic as 'Adrienne Lecouvreur,' and nothing else of M. Legouvé's is as skilful. Since the dissolution of the partnership of MM. Meilhac and Halévy they have each written alone; M. Halévy's 'Abbé Constantin' is a charming idyll, and M. Meilhac's 'Décoré' is delicately humorous; but where is the underlying strength which sustains 'Frou-frou'? where is the exuberant comic force of 'Tricoche et Cacolet'? where is the disintegrating irony of the 'Belle Hélène'? Here collaboration has proved itself. Here union has produced work finer and higher than was apparently possible to either author alone. More often than not collaboration seems accidental, and its results are not the works by which we rank either of its writers. We do not think of Charles Dickens chiefly as the author of 'No Thoroughfare,' nor is 'No Thoroughfare' the

2

book by which we judge Wilkie Collins. But 'Adrienne Lecouvreur' is the finest play on the list of
either Scribe's works or of M. Legouvé's, and ' Frou-
frou ' is the one comedy of MM. Meilhac and Halévy
likely to survive.

France is the country with the most vigorous
dramatic literature, and France is the country where
collaboration is the most frequent. The two facts
are to be set down together, without a forced suggestion that either is a consequence of the other.
But it is to be noted again that in any country where
there is a revival of the drama collaboration is likely
to become common at once. In Germany just now,
for example, there is a promising school of comedy
writers—and they are combining one with another.
In Great Britain and in the United States there are
signs of dramatic growth; and very obviously there
has been an enormous improvement in the past few
years. A comparison of the original plays written
in our language twenty-five years ago with those
now so written is most encouraging. It may seem
a little like that circular argument—which is as
dangerous as a circular saw—but I venture to suggest
that one of the causes of immediate hopefulness for
the drama in our language is the prevalence of collaboration in England and in America—for by such

partnerships the principles of play-making are spread abroad. "We learn of our contemporaries," said Emerson, "what they know, without effort, and almost through the pores of the skin." Now, a collaborator must needs be the closest of contemporaries.

With Charles Reade, Tom Taylor composed 'Masks and Faces,' an artificial comedy of undeniable effect; and with Mr. A. W. Dubourg he wrote 'New Men and Old Acres,' a comedy also artificial, but more closely akin to modern life. With Palgrave Simpson, Mr. Herman Merivale prepared a moving romantic drama, 'All for Her,' and with Mr. F. C. Grove he wrote a brilliant comedy, 'Forget-Me-Not.' To collaboration again is due the 'Silver King,' the best of recent English dramas. And collaboration, alas! is also to be credited with the most of the latest machine-made British melodramas, plays which may bear the signatures of any two of half a dozen contemporary playwrights—which reveal a most extraordinary likeness, one to the other, as though they had each been cut from the same roll of goods in lengths to suit the purchaser—and in which the pattern is always a variation of a single theme, the revengeful pursuit of an exemplary good man by an indefatigable bad man.

In America there is also an evident tendency towards co-operation, as there has been a distinct improvement in the technic of play-writing. Mr. Bronson Howard has told us that he had a silent partner in revising his 'Banker's Daughter,' known in England as the 'Old Love and the New.' To the novice in the theatre the aid of the expert is invaluable. When Mrs. Hodgson Burnett desired to make a play out of her little tale of 'Esmeralda,' she consulted counsel learned in the law of dramatic construction, Mr. William Gillette, by whose aid the comedy was written. If the poetic drama has any future on our stage, it must owe this in a measure to collaboration, for the technic of the theatre is nowadays very elaborate, and few bards are likely to master it satisfactorily. But if the poet will frankly join hands with the practical playwright, there is a hopeful possibility of success. Had Browning taken advice before he finally fixed on his action, and while the form was yet fluid, 'A Blot in the Scutcheon' might have been made a great acting play. It is while a drama is still malleable that the aid of the expert is invaluable.

The assistance which Dumas received from his frequent associates was not of this kind; it was not the co-operation of an expert partner but rather

that of a useful apprentice. The chief of these collaborators was the late Auguste Maquet, with whom
Dumas would block out the plot, and to whom he
would intrust all the toilsome detail of investigation and verification. Edmond About once caught
Dumas red-handed in the very act of collaboration,
and from his account it appears that Maquet had
set down in black and white the outline of the story
as they had developed it together, incorporating,
doubtless, his own suggestions and the result of his
historic research. This outline was contained on
little squares of paper, and each of these little
squares Dumas was amplifying into a large sheet of
manuscript in his own fine handwriting.

Thackeray answered the accusation that Dumas
did not write all his own works by asking, "Does
not the chief cook have *aides* under him? Did not
Rubens's pupils paint on his canvases?" Then—
it is in one of the most delightful passages of the
always delightful 'Roundabout Papers'—he declares
that he himself would like a competent, respectable,
and rapid clerk, to whom he might say, "Mr. Jones,
if you please, the archbishop must die this morning
in about five pages. Turn to article 'Dropsy' (or
what you will) in Encyclopædia. Take care there
are no medical blunders in his death. Group his

daughters, physicians, and chaplains round him. In Wales's ' London,' letter B, third shelf, you will find an account of Lambeth, and some prints of the place. Color in with local coloring. The daughter will come down and speak to her lover in his wherry at Lambeth Stairs." " Jones (an intelligent young man) examines the medical, historical, topographical books necessary; his chief points out to him in Jeremy Taylor (fol. London, MDCLV.) a few remarks, such as might befit a dear old archbishop departing this life. When I come back to dress for dinner the archbishop is dead on my table in five pages; medicine, topography, theology, all right, and Jones has gone home to his family some hours." This was Thackeray's whimsical suggestion; but if he had ventured to adopt it himself, I fear we should have been able to distinguish the 'prentice hand from the fine round sweep of the master.

This paper is, perhaps, rather a consideration of the principle of collaboration than an explanation of its methods. To point out the departments of literature in which collaboration may be of advantage and to indicate its more apparent limitations have been my objects, and I have postponed as long as I could any attempt to explain " how it is done." Such an explanation is at best but a doubtful possibility.

Perhaps the first requisite is a sympathy between the two partners not sufficient to make them survey life from the same point of view, but yet enough to make them respect each other's suggestions and be prepared to accept them. There is needed in both openness of mind as well as alertness, an ability to take as well as to give, a willingness to put yourself in his place and to look at the world from his standpoint. Probably it is best that the two authors shall not be too much alike in temperament. Edmond and Jules de Goncourt, for example, although not twins, thought alike on most subjects; and so close was their identity of cerebration that, when they were sitting at the same table at work on the same book, they sometimes wrote almost the same sentence at the same moment. This is collaboration carried to an abnormal and unwholesome extreme; and there is much that is morbid and much that is forced in the books the Goncourts composed together.

Collaboration may once more be likened to matrimony, and we may consider MM. Erckmann-Chatrian and Messrs. Besant and Rice as monogamists, while Scribe and Labiche, who were ready to collaborate at large, are polygamists. In marriage husband and wife are one, and that is not a happy

union when either inquires as to which one it is:
the unity should be so complete that the will of
each is merged in that of the other.   So it should
be in a literary partnership.   Respect for each other,
mutual esteem, is, perhaps, the first requisite for
collaboration as for matrimony; and good temper
is assuredly the second.

In discussing the practice of collaboration with
that past master of the art Mr. Walter Besant, he
declared to me that it was absolutely essential that
one of the two partners should be the head of the
firm.   He did not tell me who was the head of the
firm of Besant and Rice, and I have no direct testimony to offer in support of my belief that the domi-
nant member was Mr. Besant himself; but there is
a plenty of circumstantial evidence to that effect,
and, as Thoreau says, " some circumstantial evidence
is very strong—as when you find a trout in the
milk."

What Mr. Besant meant, I take it, was that there
must be a unity of impulse so that the resulting
product shall seem the outcome of a single control-
ling mind.   This may be attained by the domina-
tion of one partner, no doubt, as when Dumas
availed himself of the aid of Maquet; but it can be
the result also of an harmonious equality, as when

M. Meilhac and M. Halévy were writing together. In collaboration as in matrimony, again, it is well when the influence of the masculine element does not wholly overpower the feminine.

As there are households where husband and wife fight like cat and dog, and where marriage ends in divorce, so there are literary partnerships which are dissolved in acrimony and anger. M. Alexandre Dumas *fils* has lent his strength to the authors of the 'Supplice d'une Femme,' 'Héloïse Paranquet,' and the 'Danichef,' and there followed bad feelings and high words. Warned by this bitter experience, M. Dumas is said to have answered a request to collaborate with the query, "Why should I wish to quarrel with you?" But M. Dumas is a bad collaborator, I fancy, despite his skill and his strength. He is like the powerful ally a weak country sometimes calls in to its own undoing. Yet in his case the usual cause of disagreement between collaborators is lacking, for the plays he has recast and stamped with his own image and superscription have succeeded. Now in general it is when the work fails that the collaborators fall out. Racine made an epigram against the two now forgotten authors of a now forgotten tragedy, that each claimed it before it was produced and both renounced it after it had been acted.   The quarrels of collaborators, like the quarrels of any author, or, for that matter, like any quarrels at all to which the public are admitted, are the height of folly. The world looks on at the fight, and listens while the two former friends call each other hard names; and more often than not it believes what each says of the other, and not what he says of himself.

If I may be allowed to offer myself as a witness, I shall testify to the advantage of a literary partner-ship, which halves the labor of the task and doubles the pleasure.   It may be that I have been excep-tionally skilful in choosing my allies or exception-ally fortunate in them, but I can declare unhesitat-ingly that I have never had a hard word with a col-laborator while our work was in hand and never a bitter word with him afterwards.   My collaborators have always been my friends before and they have always remained my friends after.   Sometimes our literary partnership was the unpremeditated outcome of a friendly chat, in the course of which we chanced upon a subject, and in sport developed it until un-expectedly it seemed promising enough to be worthy of artistic consideration.   Such a subject belonged to both of us, and had best be treated by both to-gether.   There was no dispute as to our respective shares in the result of our joint labors, because we could not ourselves even guess what each had done when both had been at work together. As Augier said in the preface to the ' Lionnes Pauvres,' which he wrote with M. Edouard Foussier, we must copy " the married people who say one to the other, 'your son.' "

I have collaborated in writing stories, in making plays, and in editing books. Sometimes I may have thought that I did more than my share, sometimes I knew that I did less than I should, but always there was harmony, and never did either of us seek to assert a mastery. However done, and by whichever of the two, the subject was always thoroughly discussed between us; it was turned over and over and upside down and inside out; it was considered from all possible points of view and in every stage of development. When a final choice was made of what seemed to us best, the mere putting on paper was wholly secondary. I have written a play of which I prepared the dialogue of one act and my associate prepared that of the next; I have written a play in which I wrote the scenes in which certain characters appeared and my ally wrote those in which certain other characters appeared; I have written a short story in two chapters of which one was in my autograph and the other in my partner's; but none the less was he the half-author of the portions I set on paper, and none the less was I the half-author of the portions he set on paper.

Probably the most profitable method is that of alternate development—certainly it is for a drama. After the subject begins to take form, A makes out a tentative sequence of scenes; and this, after several talks, B fills up into an outline of the story. Slowly, and after careful consultation, A elaborates this into a detailed scenario in which every character is set forth, every entrance and every exit, with the reasons for them, every scene and every effect —in fact, everything except the words to be spoken. Then B takes this scenario, and from it he writes a first rough draft of the play itself, complete in dialogue and in "business." This rough draft A revises, and rewrites where need be. Then it goes to the copyist; and when the clean type-written manuscript returns both A and B go over it again and again, pointing and polishing, until each is satisfied with their labor in common. Perhaps the drama is the only form of literature in which so painstaking a process would be advantageous, or in which it would be advisable even; but of a play the structure can hardly be too careful or too precise, nor can the dialogue be too compact or too polished.

"I am no pickpurse of another's wit," as Sir Philip Sydney boasts, but I cannot forego the malign pleasure of quoting, in conclusion, Mr. Andrew Lang's insidious suggestion to " young men entering on the life of letters." He advises them "to find an ingenious, and industrious, and successful partner; stick to him, never quarrel with him, and do not survive him."

THE DOCUMENTS IN THE CASE.

(In Collaboration with H. C. Bunner.)

THE DOCUMENTS IN THE CASE.

I.

Document No. 1.

Paragraph from the " Illustrated London News," published under the head of " Obituary of Eminent Persons," in the issue of January 4th, 1879.

SIR WILLIAM BEAUVOIR, BART.

Sir William Beauvoir, Bart., whose lamented death has just occurred at Brighton, on December 28th, was the head and representative of the junior branch of the very ancient and honourable family of Beau voir, and was the only son of the late General Sir William Beauvoir, Bart., by his wife Anne, daughter of Colonel Doyle, of Chelsworth, Suffolk. He was born in 1805, and was educated at Eton and Trinity Hall, Cambridge. He was M.P. for Lancashire from 1837 to 1847, and was appointed a Gentleman of the Privy Chamber in 1843. Sir William married, in 1826, Henrietta Georgiana, fourth daughter of the Right Hon. Adolphus Liddell, Q.C.,

3

by whom he had two sons, William Beauvoir and Oliver Liddell Beauvoir. The latter was with his lamented parent when he died. Of the former nothing has been heard for nearly thirty years, about which time he left England suddenly for America. It is supposed that he went to California shortly after the discovery of gold. Much forgotten gossip will now in all probability be revived, for the will of the lamented baronet has been proved, on the 2d inst., and the personalty sworn under £70,000. The two sons are appointed executors. The estate in Lancashire is left to the elder, and the rest is divided between the brothers The doubt as to the career of Sir William's eldest son must now of course be cleared up.

This family of Beauvoirs is of Norman descent and of great antiquity. This is the younger branch, founded in the last century by Sir William Beauvoir, Bart., who was Chief Justice of the Canadas, whence he was granted the punning arms and motto now borne by his descendants—a beaver sable rampant on a field gules; motto, " Damno."

II.

Document No. 2.

Promises to pay put forth by William Beauvoir, junior, at various times in 1848.

> *I. O. U.*
>
> £105. 0. 0.
>
> *April* 10*th*, 1848.
>
> *William Beauvoir, junr.*

Document No. 3.
The same.

> *I. O. U.*
>
> £250. 0. 0.
>
> *April* 22*d*, 1848.
>
> *William Beauvoir, junr.*

Document No. 4.
The same.

> *I. O. U.*
>
> £600. 0. 0.
>
> *May* 10*th*, 1848.
>
> *William Beauvoir, junr.*

Document No. 5.

Extract from the " Sunday Satirist," a journal of high life published in London, May 13th, 1848.

Are not our hereditary law-makers and the members of our old families the guardians of the honour of this realm?   One would not think so to see the reckless gait at which some of them go down the road to ruin.   The D——e of D——m and the E——l of B——n and L——d Y——g,——are not these pretty guardians of a nation's name?   *Quis custodiet ?* etc.   Guardians, forsooth, *parce qu'ils se sont donnés la peine de naître !*   Some of the gentry make the running as well as their betters.   Young W——m B——r, son of old Sir W——m B——r, late M.P. for L——e, is a truly model young man.   He comes of a good old county family—his mother was a daughter of the Right Honourable A——s L— l, and he himself is old enough to know better.   But we hear of his escapades night after night and day after day.   He bets all day and he plays all night, and poor tired nature has to make the best of it. And his poor worn purse gets the worst of it.   He has duns by the score.   His I. O. U.'s are held by every Jew in the city.   He is not content with a little gentlemanlike game of whist or *écarté*, but he must needs revive for his special use and behoof the dangerous and well-nigh forgotten *pharaoh*. As luck would have it, he had lost as much at this game of brute chance as ever he would at any game of skill. His judgment of horseflesh is no better than his luck at cards. He came a cropper over the " Two Thousand Guineas." The victory of the favourite cost him to the tune of over six thousand . pounds. We learn that he hopes to recoup himself on the Derby by backing Shylock for nearly nine thousand pounds; one bet was twelve hundred guineas.

And this is the sort of man who may be chosen at any time by force of family interest to make laws for the toiling millions of Great Britain!

Document No. 6.

Extract from " Bell's Life" of May 19th, 1848.

THE DERBY DAY.

WEDNESDAY.—This day, like its predecessor, opened with a cloudless sky, and the throng which crowded the avenues leading to the grand scene of attraction was, as we have elsewhere remarked, in-calculable.

THE DERBY.

The Derby Stakes of 50 sovs. each, h. ft. for three-year-olds; colts, 8 st. 7 lb., fillies, 8 st. 2 lb.; the second to receive 100 sovs., and the winner to pay 100 sovs. towards police, etc.; mile and a half on the new Derby course; 215 subs.

Lord Clifden's b. c. Surplice, by Touchstone,	1
Mr. Bowe's b. c. Springy Jack, by Hetman,	2
Mr. B. Green's br. c. Shylock, by Simoon,	3
Mr. Payne's b. c. Glendower, by Slane,	0
Mr. J. P. Day's b. c. Nil Desperandum, by Venison,	0

Document No. 7.

Paragraph of Shipping Intelligence from the Liverpool "Courier" of June 21st, 1848.

The bark *Euterpe*, Captain Riding, belonging to the Transatlantic Clipper Line of Messrs. Judkins & Cooke, left the Mersey yesterday afternoon, bound for New York. She took out the usual complement of steerage passengers. The first officer's cabin is occupied by Professor Titus Peebles, M.R.C.S., M.R.G.S., lately instructor in metallurgy at the University of Edinburgh, and Mr. William Beauvoir. Professor Peebles, we are informed, has an important scientific mission in the States and will not return for six months.

Document No. 8.

Paragraph from the New York " Herald" of September 9th, 1848.

While we well know that the record of vice and dissipation can never be pleasing to the refined tastes of the cultivated denizens of the only morally pure metropolis on the face of the earth, yet it may be of interest to those who enjoy the fascinating study of human folly and frailty to " point a moral or adorn a tale " from the events transpiring in our very midst. Such as these will view with alarm the sad example afforded the youth of our city by the dissolute career of a young lump of aristocratic affectation and patrician profligacy, recently arrived in this city. This young *gentleman's* (save the mark!) name is Lord William F. Beauvoir, the latest scion of a venerable and wealthy English family. We print the full name of this beautiful exemplar of " haughty Albion," although he first appeared among our citizens under the alias of Beaver, by which name he is now generally known, although recorded on the books of the Astor House by the name which our enterprise first gives to the public. Lord Beauvoir's career since his arrival here has been one of unexampled extravagance and mad im-

morality.   His days and nights have been passed in
the gilded palaces of the fickle goddess Fortune in
Thomas Street and College Place, where he has
squandered fabulous sums, by some stated to amount
to over £78,000 sterling.   It is satisfactory to know
that retribution has at last overtaken him.   His
enormous income has been exhausted to the ultimate farthing, and at latest accounts he had quit
the city, leaving behind him, it is shrewdly suspected, a large hotel bill, though no such admission
can be extorted from his last landlord, who is evidently a sycophantic adulator of British "aristocracy."

Document No. 9.

*Certificate of Deposit, vulgarly known as a pawn-
ticket, issued by one Simpson to William Beauvoir,
December 2d, 1848.*

John Simpson,
Loan Office,
36 Bowery,
New York.

Dec. 2d, 1848.

	Dolls.	Cts.
One Gold Hunting-case Watch and Chain,	150	00
William Beauvoir.		

Not accountable in case of fire, damage, moth, robbery, breakage, &c.   25
per cent. per ann.   Good for 1 year only.

Document No. 10.

Letter from the late John Phœnix, found among the posthumous papers of the late John P. Squibob, and promptly published in the San Diego " Herald."

OFF THE COAST OF FLORIDA, January 3d, 1849.

MY DEAR SQUIB:—I imagine your pathetic inquiry as to my whereabouts—pathetic, not to say hypothetic—for I am now where I cannot hear the dulcet strains of your voice. I am on board ship. I am half seas over. I am bound for California by way of the Isthmus. I am going for the gold, my boy, the gold. In the mean time I am lying around loose on the deck of this magnificent vessel, the *Mercy G. Tarbox*, of Nantucket, bred by *Noah's Ark* out of *Pilot-boat*, dam by *Mudscow* out of *Raging Canawl*. The *Mercy G. Tarbox* is one of the best boats of Nantucket, and Captain Clearstarch is one of the best captains all along shore — although, friend Squibob, I feel sure that you are about to observe that a captain with a name like that would give any one the blues. But don't do it, Squib! Spare me this once.

But as a matter of fact this ultramarine joke of yours is about east. It was blue on the *Mercy G.* — mighty blue, too. And it needed the inspiring hope of the gold I was soon to pick up in nuggets to stiffen my backbone to a respectable degree of rigidity. I was about ready to wilt. But I discovered two Englishmen on board, and now I get along all right. We have formed a little temperance society—just we three, you know—to see if we cannot, by a course of sampling and severe study, discover which of the captain's liquors is most dangerous, so that we can take the pledge not to touch it. One of them is a chemist or a metallurgist, or something scientific. The other is a gentleman.

The chemist or metallurgist or something scientific is Professor Titus Peebles, who is going out to prospect for gold. He feels sure that his professional training will give him the inside track in the gulches and gold mines. He is a smart chap. He invented the celebrated "William Riley Baking Powder"—bound to rise up every time.

And here I must tell you a little circumstance. As I was coming down to the dock in New York, to go aboard the *Mercy G.*, a small boy was walloping a boy still smaller; so I made peace, and walloped them both. And then they both began heaving rocks at me, one of which I caught dexterously in the dexter hand. Yesterday, as I was pacing the deck with the professor, I put my hand in my pocket and found this stone. So I asked the professor what it was.

He looked at it and said it was gneiss.

"Is it?" said I. "Well, if a small but energetic youth had taken you on the back of the head with it, you would not think it so nice!"

And then, O Squib, he set out to explain that he meant "gneiss," not "nice!" The ignorance of these English about a joke is really wonderful. It is easy to see that they have never been brought up on them. But perhaps there was some excuse for the professor that day, for he was the president *pro tem.* of our projected temperance society, and as such he had been making a quantitative and qualitative analysis of another kind of quarts.

So much for the chemist or metallurgist or something scientific. The gentleman and I get on better. His name is Beaver, which he persists in spelling Beauvoir. Ridiculous, isn't it? How easy it is to see that the English have never had the advantage of a good common-school education—so few of them can spell. Here's a man don't know how to spell his own name. And this shows how the race over there on the little island is degenerating. It was not so in other days. Shakespeare, for instance, not only knew how to spell his own name, but—and

this is another proof of his superiority to his contemporaries—he could spell it in half a dozen different ways.

This Beaver is a clever fellow, and we get on first
rate together. He is going to California for gold —
like the rest of us. But I think he has had his share
—and spent it. At any rate he has not much now.
I have been teaching him poker, and I am afraid
he won't have any soon. I have an idea he has
been going pretty fast—and mostly down hill. But
he has his good points. He is a gentleman all
through, as you can see. Yes, friend Squibob, even
you could see right through him. We are all going
to California together, and I wonder which one of
the three will turn up trumps first—Beaver, or the
chemist, metallurgist or something scientific, or

   Yours respectfully, JOHN PHŒNIX.

P. S.—You think this a stupid letter, perhaps, and
not interesting. Just reflect on my surroundings.
Besides, the interest will accumulate a good while
before you get the missive. And I don't know how
you ever are to get it, for there is no post-office near
here, and on the Isthmus the mails are as uncertain
as the females are everywhere. (I am informed that
there is no postage on old jokes—so I let that stand.)

       J. P.

Document No. 11.

Extract from the Bone Gulch "Palladium," June 3d, 1850.

Our readers may remember hovv frequeñtly vve have declared our firm belief in the future uñex-ampled prosperity of Boñe Gulch. VVe savv it in the immediate future the metropolis of the Pacific Slope, as it was intended by nature to be. VVe poiñted out repeatedly that a time vvould come vvheñ Bone Gulch would be an emporium of the arts and sciences añd of the best society, even more thañ it is novv. VVe foresavv the time vvheñ the best men from the old cities of the East vvould come flocking to us, passing vvith coñtempt the puñy settlement of Deadhorse. But eveñ vve did not so soon see that members of the aristocracy of the effete monarchies of despotic Europe vvould ackñovvledge the undeniable advantages of Boñe Gulch, and come here to stay permanently añd for-ever. VVithiñ the past vveek vve have received here Hon. VVilliam Beaver, one of the first men of Great Britain añd Ireland, a statesman, an orator, a soldier, and an exteñsive traveller. He has come to Bone Gulch as the best spot oñ the face of the everlasting uñiverse. It is needless to say that our prominent citizens have received him with great cordiality. Bone Gulch is not like Deadhorse. VVe knovv a gentleman vvhen vve see one.

Hon. Mr. Beaver is one of nature's noblemen; he is also related to the Royal Family of England. He is a second cousin of the Queen, and boards at the Tovver of London vvith her vvhen at home. VVe are informed that he has frequently taken the Prince of VVales out for a ride in his baby-vvagon.

VVe take great pleasure in congratulating Bone Gulch on its latest acquisition. And we knovv Hon. Mr. Beaver is sure to get along all right here under the best climate in the vvorld and vvith the noblest men the sun ever shone on.

Document No. 12.

Extract from the Dead Horse " Gazette and Courier of Civilization " of August 26th, 1850.

BONEGULCH'S BRITISHER.

Bonegulch sits in sackcloth and ashes and cools her mammoth cheek in the breezes of Colorado Canyon. The self-styled Emporium of the West has lost her British darling, Beaver Bill, the big swell who was first cousin to the Marquis of Buckingham and own grandmother to the Emperor of China,

the man with the biled shirt and low-necked shoes.
This curled darling of the Bonegulch aristocrat-
worshippers passed through Deadhorse yesterday,
clean bust. Those who remember how the four-fin-
gered editor of the Bonegulch *Palladium* pricked
up his ears and lifted up his falsetto crow when this
lovely specimen of the British snob first honored
him by striking him for a $ will appreciate the point
of the joke.

It is said that the *Palladium* is going to come
out, when it makes its next semi-occasional appearance, in full mourning, with turned rules. For this
festive occasion we offer Brother B. the use of our
late retired Spanish font, which we have discarded
for the new and elegant dress in which we appear to-
day and to which we have elsewhere called the attention of our readers. It will be a change for the
Palladium's eleven unhappy readers, who are getting
very tired of the old type cast for the Concha
Mission in 1811, which tries to make up for its lack
of w's by a plentiful superfluity of greaser v's. How
are you, Brother Biles?

"We don't know a gent when we see him." Oh
no (?)!

.

Document No. 13.

Paragraph from " Police Court Notes," in the New Centreville [late Dead Horse] " Evening Gazette," January 2d, 1858.

HYMENEAL HIGH JINKS.

William Beaver, better known ten years ago as " Beaver Bill," is now a quiet and prosperous agriculturist in the Steal Valley. He was, however, a pioneer in the 1849 movement, and a vivid memory of this fact at times moves him to quit his bucolic labors and come in town for a real old-fashioned tare. He arrived in New Centreville during Christmas week and got married suddenly, but not unexpectedly, yesterday morning. His friends took it upon themselves to celebrate the joyful occasion, rare in the experience of at least one of the parties, by getting very high on Irish Ike's whiskey and serenading the newly-married couple with fish-horns, horse-fiddles, and other improvised musical instruments. Six of the participators in this epithalamial serenade, namely, José Tanco, Hiram Scuttles, John P. Jones, Hermann Bumgardner, Jean Durant (" Frenchy "), and Bernard McGinnis (" Big Barney "), were taken in tow by the police force, assisted by citizens, and locked up over night, to cool their generous enthusiasm in the gloomy dungeons of Justice Skinner's calaboose. This morning all were discharged with a reprimand, except Big Barney and José Tanco, who, being still drunk, were allotted ten days in default of $10. The bridal pair left this noon for the bridegroom's ranch.

Document No. 14.

Extract from the New York "Herald" for June 23d, 1861.

THE REDSKINS.

A BORDER WAR AT LAST.

INDIAN INSURRECTION.

RED DEVILS RISING.

WOMEN AND CHILDREN SEEKING SAFETY IN THE LARGER TOWNS.

HORRIBLE HOLOCAUSTS ANTICIPATED.

BURYING THE HATCHET—IN THE WHITE MAN'S HEAD.

[SPECIAL DISPATCH TO THE NEW YORK HERALD.]

CHICAGO, June 22, 1861.

Great uneasiness exists all along the Indian frontier. Nearly all the regular troops have been with-

4

drawn from the West for service in the South.
With the return of the warm weather it seems certain that the redskins will take advantage of the
opportunity thus offered, and inaugurate a bitter
and vindictive fight against the whites. Rumors
come from the agencies that the Indians are leaving
in numbers. A feverish excitement among them
has been easily to be detected. Their ponies are
now in good condition, and forage can soon be had
in abundance on the prairie, if it is not already.
Everything points towards a sudden and startling
outbreak of hostilities.

[SPECIAL DISPATCH TO THE NEW YORK HERALD.]
ST. PAUL, June 22, 1861.

The Sioux near here are all in a ferment. Experienced Indian fighters say the signs of a speedy
going on the war-path are not to be mistaken. No
one can tell how soon the whole frontier may be in
a bloody blaze. The women and children are rapidly coming in from all exposed settlements. Nothing overt as yet has transpired, but that the Indians
will collide very soon with the settlers is certain.
All the troops have been withdrawn. In our de-
fenceless state there is no knowing how many lives
may be lost before the regiments of volunteers now
organizing can take the field.

LATER.

THE WAR BEGUN.

FIRST BLOOD FOR THE INDIANS.

The Scalping-Knife and the Tomahawk at work again.

[special dispatch to the new york herald.]

Black Wing Agency, June 22, 1861.

The Indians made a sudden and unexpected attack on the town of Coyote Hill, forty miles from here, last night, and did much damage before the surprised settlers rallied and drove them off. The redskins met with heavy losses. Among the whites killed are a man named William Beaver, sometimes called Beaver Bill, and his wife. Their child, a beautiful little girl of two, was carried off by the red rascals. A party has been made up to pursue them. Owing to their taking their wounded with them, the trail is very distinct.

Document No. 15.

Letter from Mrs. Edgar Saville, in San Francisco,
to Mr. Edgar Saville, in Chicago.

CAL. JARDINE'S

MONSTER VARIETY AND DRAMATIC COMBINATION.
ON THE ROAD.

G. W. K. McCULLUM, *Treasurer.* *HI. SAMUELS,* *Stage Manager.* *JNO. SHANKS,* *Advance.*	*No dates filled except with first-class houses.* *Hall owners will please consider silence a polite negative.*

SAN FRANCISCO, January 29, 1863.

MY DEAR OLD MAN!—Here we are in our second
week at Frisco and you will be glad to know playing to steadily increasing biz, having signed for two
weeks more, certain. I didn't like to mention it
when I wrote you last, but things were very queer
after we left Denver, and " Treasury " was a mock-
ery till we got to Bluefoot Springs, which is a mining town, where we showed in the hotel dining-room.
Then there was a strike just before the curtain went
up. The house was mostly miners in red shirts and
very exacting. The sinews were forthcoming very
quick my dear, and after that the ghost walked
quite regular. So now everything is bright, and
you won't have to worry if Chicago doesn't do the
right thing by you.

I don't find this engagement half as disagreeable as I expected. Of course it ain't so very nice travelling in a combination with variety talent but they keep to themselves and we regular professionals make a *happy family* that Barnum would not be ashamed of and quite separate and comfortable. We don't associate with any of them only with The Unique Mulligan's wife, because he beats her. So when he is on a regular she sleeps with me.

And talking of liquor dear old man, if you knew how glad and proud I was to see you writing so straight and steady and beautiful in your three last letters. O, I'm sure my darling if the boys thought of the little wife out on the road they wouldn't plague you so with the Enemy. Tell Harry Atkinson this from me, he has a good kind heart but he is the worst of your friends. Every night when I am dressing I think of you at Chicago, and pray you may never again go on the way you did that terrible night at Rochester. Tell me dear, did you look handsome in Horatio? You ought to have had Laertes instead of that duffing Merivale.

And now I have the queerest thing to tell you. Jardine is going in for Indians and has secured six very ugly ones. I mean real Indians, not professional. They are hostile Comanshies or something who have just laid down their arms. They had an insurrection in the first year of the War, when the troops went East, and they killed all the settlers and ranches and destroyed the canyons somewhere out in Nevada, and when they were brought here they had a wee little kid with them only four or five years old, but *so sweet.* They stole her and killed her parents and brought her up for their own in the cunningest little moccasins. She could not speak a word of English except her own name which is Nina. She has blue eyes and all her second teeth. The ladies here made a great fuss about her and sent her flowers and worsted afgans, but they did not do anything else for her and left her to us.

O dear old man you must let me have her! You never refused me a thing yet and she is so like our Avonia Marie that my heart almost breaks when she puts her arms around my neck—*she calls me mamma already.* I want to have her with us when we get the little farm—and it must be near, that little farm of ours—we have waited for it so long— and something tells me my own old faker will make his hit soon and be great. You can't tell how I have loved it and hoped for it and how real every foot of that farm is to me. And though I can never see my own darling's face among the roses it will make me

so happy to see this poor dead mother's pet get red
and rosy in the country air.   And till the farm
comes we shall always have enough for her, without
your ever having to black up again as you did for
me the winter I was sick my own poor boy!

Write me yes—you will be glad when you see her.
And now love and regards to Mrs. Barry and all
friends.   Tell the Worst of Managers that he knows
where to find his leading juvenile for next season.
Think how funny it would be for us to play together next year—we haven't done it since '57—the
third year we were married.   That was my first
season higher than walking—and now I'm quite an
old woman—most thirty dear!

Write me soon a letter like that last one—and
send a kiss to Nina—*our Nina.*

Your own girl,

MARY.

P. S.   He has not worried me since.

Nina drew this herself she says it is a horse so
that you can get here soon.

III.

Document No. 16.

Letter from Messrs. Throstlethwaite, Throstlethwaite, and Dick, Solicitors, Lincoln's Inn, London, England, to Messrs. Hitchcock and Van Rensselaer, Attorneys and Counsellors at Law, 76 Broadway, New York, U. S. A.

January 8, 1879.

MESSRS. HITCHCOCK AND VAN RENSSELAER.

GENTLEMEN: On the death of our late client, Sir William Beauvoir, Bart., and after the reading of the deceased gentleman's will, drawn up nearly forty years ago by our Mr. Dick, we were requested by Oliver Beauvoir, Esq., the second son of the late Sir William, to assist him in discovering and communicating with his elder brother, the present Sir William Beauvoir, of whose domicile we have little or no information.

After a consultation between Mr. Oliver Beauvoir and our Mr. Dick, it was seen that the sole knowledge in our possession amounted substantially to this: Thirty years ago the elder son of the late baronet, after indulging in dissipation in every possible form, much to the sorrow of his respected parent,

who frequently expressed as much to our Mr. Dick,
disappeared, leaving behind him bills and debts of
all descriptions, which we, under instructions from
Sir William, examined, audited, and paid. Sir William Beauvoir would allow no search to be made for
his erring son and would listen to no mention of his
name. Current gossip declared that he had gone to
New York, where he probably arrived about mid-
summer, 1848. Mr. Oliver Beauvoir thinks that he
crossed to the States in company with a distinguished scientific gentleman, Professor Titus Peebles.
Within a year after his departure news came that
he had gone to California with Professor Peebles;
this was about the time gold was discovered in the
States. That the present Sir William Beauvoir did
about this time actually arrive on the Pacific Coast
in company with the distinguished scientific man
above mentioned, we have every reason to believe:
we have even direct evidence on the subject. A
former junior clerk, who had left us at about the
same period as the disappearance of the elder son
of our late client, accosted our Mr. Dick when the
latter was in Paris last summer, and informed him
(our Mr. Dick) that he (the former junior clerk) was
now a resident of Nevada and a member of Con-
gress for that county, and in the course of conver-

sation he mentioned that he had seen Professor
Peebles and the son of our late client in San Francisco, nearly thirty years ago.   Other information
we have none.   It ought not to be difficult to discover Professor Peebles, whose scientific attainments have doubtless ere this been duly recognized
by the U. S. government.   As our late client leaves
the valuable family estate in Lancashire to his elder
son and divides the remainder equally between his
two sons, you will readily see why we invoke your
assistance in discovering the present domicile of the
late baronet's elder son, or, in default thereof, in
placing in our hand such proof of his death as may
be necessary to establish that lamentable fact in our
probate court.

We have the honor to remain, as ever, your most
humble and obedient servants,

THROSTLETHWAITE, THROSTLETHWAITE, AND DICK.

P. S.—Our late client's grandson, Mr. William
Beauvoir, the only child of Oliver Beauvoir, Esq.,
is now in the States, in Chicago or Nebraska or
somewhere in the West.   We shall be pleased if
you can keep him informed as to the progress of
your investigations.   Our Mr. Dick has requested
Mr. Oliver Beauvoir to give his son your address,

and to suggest his calling on you as he passes through New York on his way home.

T. T. & D.

Document No. 17.

Letter from Messrs. Hitchcock and Van Rensselaer, New York, to Messrs. Pixley and Sutton, Attorneys and Counsellors at Law, 98 California Street, San Francisco, California.

Law Offices of Hitchcock & Van Rensselaer,
76 Broadway, New York.
P. O. Box 4076.

Jan. 22, 1879.

MESSRS. PIXLEY & SUTTON.

GENTLEMEN:—We have just received from our London correspondents, Messrs. Throstlethwaite, Throstlethwaite, and Dick, of Lincoln's Inn, London, the letter, a copy of which is herewith inclosed, to which we invite your attention. We request that you will do all in your power to aid us in the search for the missing Englishman. From the letter of Messrs. Throstlethwaite, Throstlethwaite, and Dick, it seems extremely probable, not to say certain, that Mr. Beauvoir arrived in your city about 1849, in company with a distinguished English scientist, Professor Titus Peebles, whose professional attainments were such that he is probably well known, if not in California, at least in some other of the mining States. The first thing to be done, therefore, it seems to us, is to ascertain the whereabouts of the professor, and to interview him at once. It may be that he has no knowledge of the present domicile of Mr. William Beauvoir, in which case we shall rely on you to take such steps as, in your judgment, will best conduce to a satisfactory solution of the mystery. In any event, please look up Professor Peebles and interview him at once.

Pray keep us fully informed by telegraph of your movements   Yr obt serv'ts,

HITCHCOCK & VAN RENSSELAER.

Document No. 18.

Telegram from Messrs. Pixley and Sutton, Attorneys and Counsellors at Law, 98 California Street, San Francisco, California, to Messrs. Hitchcock and Van Rensselaer, Attorneys and Counsellors at Law, 76 Broadway, New York.

SAN FRANCISCO, CAL., Jan. 30.

Tite Peebles well known frisco not professor keeps faro bank.

PIXLEY & SUTTON.   (D. H. 919.)

Document No. 19.

Telegram from Messrs. Hitchcock and Van Rensselaer to Messrs. Pixley and Sutton, in answer to the preceding.

NEW YORK, Jan. 30.

Must be mistake Titus Peebles distinguished scientist.

HITCHCOCK & VAN RENSSELAER.

(Free. Answer to D. H.)

Document No. 20.

Telegram from Messrs. Pixley and Sutton to Messrs. Hitchcock and Van Rensselaer, in reply to the preceding.

SAN FRANCISCO, CAL., Jan. 30.

No mistake distinguished faro banker suspected skin game shall we interview.

PIXLEY & SUTTON.   (D. H. 919.)

Document No. 21.

Telegram from Messrs. Hitchcock and Van Rensselaer to Messrs. Pixley and Sutton, in reply to the preceding.

NEW YORK, Jan. 30.

Must be mistake interview anyway.

HITCHCOCK & VAN RENSSELAER.

(Free. Answer to D. H.)

Document No. 22.

Telegram from Messrs. Pixley and Sutton to Messrs. Hitchcock and Van Rensselaer, in reply to the preceding.

SAN FRANCISCO, CAL., Jan. 30

Peebles out of town have written him.

PIXLEY & SUTTON.   (D. H. 919.)

Document No. 23.

Letter from Tite W. Peebles, delegate to the California Constitutional Convention, Sacramento, to Messrs. Pixley and Sutton, 98 California Street, San Francisco, California.

SACRAMENTO, Feb. 2, '79.

MESSRS. PIXLEY & SUTTON, San Francisco.

GENTLEMEN:—Your favor of the 31st ult., forwarded me from San Francisco, has been duly rec'd, and contents thereof noted.

My time is at present so fully occupied by my duties as a delegate to the Constitutional Convention that I can only jot down a brief report of my recollections on this head. When I return to S. F., I shall be happy to give you any further information that may be in my possession.

The person concerning whom you inquire was my fellow-passenger on my first voyage to this State on board the *Mercy G. Tarbox*, in the latter part of the year. He was then known as Mr. William Beauvoir. I was acquainted with his history, of which the details escape me at this writing. He was a countryman of mine; a member of an important county family—Devonian, I believe—and had left England on account of large gambling debts, of which he confided to me the exact figure. I believe they totted up something like £14,500.

I had at no time a very intimate acquaintance with Mr. Beauvoir; during our sojourn on the *Tarbox* he was the chosen associate of a depraved and vicious character named Phœnix. I am not averse from saying that I was then a member of a profession rather different to my present one, being, in fact, professor of metallurgy, and I saw much less, at that period, of Mr. B. than I probably should now.

Directly we landed at S. F., the object of your inquiries set out for the gold region, without adequate preparation, like so many others did at that time, and, I heard, fared very ill.

I encountered him some six months later; I have forgotten precisely in what locality, though I have a faint impression that his then habitat was some canyon or ravine deriving its name from certain os-

seous deposits.   Here he had engaged in the business of gold-mining, without, perhaps, sufficient
grounds for any confident hope of ultimate success.
I have his I. O. U. for the amount of my fee for
assaying several specimens from his claim, said specimens being all iron pyrites.

This is all I am able to call to mind at present in
the matter of Mr. Beauvoir.   I trust his subsequent
career was of a nature better calculated to be satisfactory to himself; but his mineralogical knowledge
was but superficial; and his character was sadly
deformed by a fatal taste for low associates.

I remain, gentlemen, your very humble and obd't
servant,   TITUS W. PEEBLES.

P. S.—Private.

MY DEAR PIX:—If you don't feel inclined to pony
up that little sum you are out on the bay gelding,
drop down to my place when I get back and I'll
give you another chance for your life at the paste-
boards.   Constitution going through.

Yours,   TITE.

IV.

Document No. 24.

Extract from the New Centreville [late Dead Horse] " Gazette and Courier of Civilization," December 20th, 1878.

Miss Nina Saville appeared last night at the Mendocino Grand Opera House, in her unrivalled specialty of *Winona, the Child of the Prairies;* supported by Tompkins and Frobisher's Grand Stellar Constellation. Although Miss Saville has long been known as one of the most promising of California's young tragediennes, we feel safe in saying that the impression she produced upon the large and cultured audience gathered to greet her last night stamped her as one of the greatest and most phenomenal geniuses of our own or other times. Her marvellous beauty of form and feature, added to her wonderful artistic power, and her perfect mastery of the difficult science of clog-dancing, won her an immediate place in the hearts of our citizens, and confirmed the belief that California need no longer look to Europe or Chicago for dramatic talent of the highest order. The sylphlike beauty, the harmonious and ever-varying grace, the vivacity and the power of the young artist who made her maiden effort among us last night, prove conclusively that the virgin soil of California teems with yet undiscovered fires of genius. The drama of *Winona, the Child of the Prairies*, is a pure, refined, and thoroughly absorbing entertainment, and has been pronounced by the entire press of the country equal to if not superior to the fascinating *Lady of Lyons*. It introduces all the favorites of the company in new and original characters, and with its original music, which is a prominent

5

feature, has already received over 200 representations in the
principal cities in the country. It abounds in effective situa-
tions, striking tableaux, and a most quaint and original
concert entitled " The Mule Fling," which alone is worth the
price of admission. As this is the first presentation in this
city, the theatre will, no doubt, be crowded, and seats will be
secured early in the day. The drama will be preceded by
that prince of humorists, Mr. Billy Barker, in his humorous
sketches and pictures from life.

We quote the above from our esteemed contemporary, the Mendocino *Gazette*, at the request of
Mr. Zeke Kilburn, Miss Saville's advance agent, who
has still further appealed to us, not only on the
ground of our common humanity, but as the only
appreciative and thoroughly-informed critics on the
Pacific Slope, to "indorse" this rather vivid expression of opinion. Nothing will give us greater pleasure. Allowing for the habitual enthusiasm of our
northern neighbor, and for the well-known chaste
aridity of Mendocino in respect of female beauty,
we have no doubt that Miss Nina Saville is all that
the fancy, peculiarly opulent and active even for an
advance agent, of Mr. Kilburn has painted her, and
is quite such a vision of youth, beauty, and artistic
phenomenality as will make the stars of Paris and
Illinois pale their ineffectual fires.

Miss Saville will appear in her " unrivalled specialty" at Hanks' New Centreville Opera House to-morrow night, as may be gathered, in a general way, from an advertisement in another column.

We should not omit to mention that Mr. Zeke Kilburn, Miss Saville's advance agent, is a gentleman of imposing presence, elegant manners, and complete knowledge of his business. This information may be relied upon as at least authentic, having been derived from Mr. Kilburn himself, to which we can add, as our own contribution, the statement that Mr. Kilburn is a gentleman of marked liberality in his ideas of spirituous refreshments, and of equal originality in his conception of the uses, objects, and personal susceptibilities of the journalistic profession.

Document No. 25.

Local item from the New Centreville "Standard," December 20th, 1878.

Hon. William Beauvoir has registered at the United States Hotel. Mr. Beauvoir is a young English gentleman of great wealth, now engaged in investigating the gigantic resources of this great country. We welcome him to New Centreville.

Document No. 26.

Programme of the performance given in the Centreville Theatre, December 21st, 1878.

HANKS' NEW CENTREVILLE OPERA HOUSE.

A. JACKSON HANKS......... Sole Proprietor and Manager.

FIRST APPEARANCE IN THIS CITY OF

TOMPKINS & FROBISHER'S

GRAND STELLAR CONSTELLATION,

Supporting California's favorite daughter, the young American
Tragedienne,

MISS NINA SAVILLE,

Who will appear in Her Unrivalled Specialty,

"WINONA, THE CHILD OF THE PRAIRIE."

THIS EVENING, DECEMBER 21st, 1878,

Will be presented, with the following phenomenal cast, the accepted
American Drama,

WINONA, THE CHILD OF THE PRAIRIE.

WINONA......	
Miss FLORA MacMADISON...	
BIDDY FLAHERTY...	Miss NINA
OLD AUNT DINAH (with Song, "Don't Get Weary")...	SAVILLE.
SALLY HOSKINS (with the old-time melody, "Bobbin' Around")...	
POOR JOE (with Song)...	
FRAULINELINA BOOBENSTEIN (with stammering Song,"I yoost landet"...	
SIR EDMOND BENNET (specially engaged)......E. C. GRAINGER	
WALTON TRAVERS......G. W. PARSONS	
GIPSY JOE......M. ISAACS	
'ANNABLE 'ORACE 'IGGINS......BILLY BARKER	
TOMMY TIPPER......Miss MAMIE SMITH	
PETE, the Man on the Dock......SI HANCOCK	
Mrs. MALONE, the Old Woman in the Little House......Mrs. K. Y. BOOTH	
ROBERT BENNETT (aged 5)......LITTLE ANNIE WATSON	

Act I.—The Old Home. Act II.—Alone in the World.

Act III.—The Frozen Gulf:

THE GREAT ICEBERG SENSATION.

Act IV.—Wedding Bells.

"WINONA, THE CHILD OF THE PRAIRIE," WILL BE PRECEDED BY

A FAVORITE FARCE,

In which the great BILLY BARKER will appear in one of his most outrage-
ously funny bits.

NEW SCENERY by Q. Z. SLOCUM.
Music by Professor Kiddoo's Silver Bugle Brass Band and
Philharmonic Orchestra.

Chickway's Grand Piano, lent by Schmidt, 2 Opera House Block.

AFTER THE SHOW GO TO HANKS' AND SEE A MAN!

Pop Williams, the only legitimate Bill-Poster in New Centreville.

(New Centreville Standard Print.)

Document No. 27.

Extract from the New Centreville [late Dead Horse] "Gazette and Courier of Civilization," December 24th, 1878.

A little while ago, in noting the arrival of Miss Nina Saville, at the New Centreville Opera House, we quoted rather extensively from our esteemed contemporary, the Mendocino *Times*, and commented upon the quotation. Shortly afterwards, it may also be remembered, we made a very direct and decided apology for the sceptical levity which inspired those remarks, and expressed our hearty sympathy with the honest, if somewhat effusive, enthusiasm with which the dramatic critic of Mendocino greeted the sweet and dainty little girl who threw over the dull, weary old business of the stage "sensation" the charm of a fresh and childlike beauty and originality, as rare and delicate as those strange, unreasonable little glimmers of spring sunsets that now and then light up for a brief moment the dull skies of winter evenings, and seem to have strayed into ungrateful January out of sheer pity for the sad earth.

Mendocino noticed the facts that form the basis of the above meteorological simile, and we believe we gave Mendocino full credit for it at the time.

We refer to the matter at this date only because in our remarks of a few days ago we had occasion to mention the fact of the existence of Mr. Zeke Kilburn, an advance agent, who called upon us at the time, to endeavor to induce us, by means apparently calculated more closely for the latitude of Mendocino, to extend to Miss Saville, before her appearance, the critical approbation which we gladly extended after. This little item of interest we alluded to at the time, and furthermore intimated, with some vagueness, that there existed in Mr. Kilburn's character a certain misdirected zeal which, combined with a too keen artistic appreciation, are apt to be rather dangerous stock in trade for an advance agent.

It was twenty-seven minutes past two o'clock yesterday afternoon. The chaste white mystery of Shigo Mountain was already taking on a faint, almost imperceptible hint of pink, like the warm cheek of a girl who hears a voice and anticipates a blush. Yet the rays of the afternoon sun rested with undiminished radiance on the empty pork-barrel in front of McMullin's shebang. A small and vagrant infant, whose associations with empty barrels were doubtless hitherto connected solely with dreams of saccharine dissipation, approached the bung-hole

with precocious caution, and retired with celerity
and a certain acquisition of experience. An unat-
tached goat, a martyr to the radical theory of personal investigation, followed in the footsteps of
infantile humanity, retired with even greater prompt-
itude, and was fain to stay its stomach on a presum-
ably empty rend-rock can, afterwards going into seclusion behind McMullin's horse-shed, before the
diuretic effect of tin flavored with blasting-powder
could be observed by the attentive eye of science.

Mr. Kilburn emerged from the hostelry of McMullin. Mr. Kilburn, as we have before stated at his
own request, is a gentleman of imposing presence.
It is well that we made this statement when we did,
for it is hard to judge of the imposing quality in a
gentleman's presence when that gentleman is sus-
pended from the arm of another gentleman by the
collar of the first gentleman's coat. The gentleman
in the rear of Mr. Kilburn was Mr. William Beauvoir, a young Englishman in a check suit. Mr.
Beauvoir is not avowedly a man of imposing presence; he wears a seal ring, and he is generally a
scion of an effete oligarchy, but he has, since his introduction into this community, behaved himself, to
use the adjectival adverb of Mr. McMullin, *white*,
and he has a very remarkable biceps. These quali-

ties may hereafter enhance his popularity in New Centreville.

Mr. Beauvoir's movements, at twenty-seven minutes past two yesterday afternoon, were few and simple. He doubled Mr. Kilburn up, after the fashion of an ordinary jack-knife, and placed him in the barrel, wedge-extremity first, remarking, as he did so, "She is, is she?" He then rammed Mr. Kilburn carefully home and put the cover on.

We learn to-day that Mr. Kilburn has resumed his professional duties on the road.

Document No. 28.

Account of the same event, from the New Centreville "Standard," December 24th, 1878.

It seems strange that even the holy influences which radiate from this joyous season cannot keep some men from getting into unseemly wrangles. It was only yesterday that our local saw a street row here in the quiet avenues of our peaceful city— a street row recalling the riotous scenes which took place here before Dead Horse experienced a change of heart and became New Centreville. Our local succeeded in gathering all the particulars of the affray, and the following statement is reliable. It seems that Mr. Kilburn, the gentlemanly and affable

advance agent of the Nina Saville Dramatic Company, now performing at Andy Hanks' Opera House
to big houses, was brutally assaulted by a ruffianly
young Englishman, named Beauvoir, for no cause
whatever. We say for no cause, as it is obvious
that Mr. Kilburn, as the agent of the troupe, could
have said nothing against Miss Saville which an
outsider, not to say a foreigner like Mr. Beauvoir,
had any call to resent. Mr. Kilburn is a gentleman
unaccustomed to rough-and-tumble encounters,
while his adversary has doubtless associated more
with pugilists than gentlemen—at least any one
would think so from his actions yesterday. Beauvoir
hustled Mr. Kilburn out of Mr. McMullin's, where
the unprovoked assault began, and violently shook
him across the new plank sidewalk. The person by
the name of Clark, whom Judge Jones for some
reason now permits to edit the moribund but once
respectable *Gazette*, caught the eye of the congenial
Beauvoir, and, true to the ungentlemanly instincts
of his base nature, pointed to a barrel in the street.
The brutal Englishman took the hint and thrust Mr.
Kilburn forcibly into the barrel, leaving the vicinity
before Mr. Kilburn, emerging from his close quar-
ters, had fully recovered. What the ruffianly Beauvoir's motive may have been for this wanton assault

it is impossible to say; but it is obvious to all why this fellow Clark sought to injure Mr. Kilburn, a gentleman whose many good qualities he of course fails to appreciate. Mr. Kilburn, recognizing the acknowledged merits of our job office, had given us the contract for all the printing he needed in New Centreville.

Document No. 29.

Advertisement from the New York "Clipper," December 21st, 1878.

WINSTON & MACK'S

GRAND INTERNATIONAL

MEGATHERIUM VARIETY COMBINATION.

COMPANY CALL.

Ladies and Gentlemen of the Company will assemble for rehearsal at Emerson's Opera House, San Francisco, on Wednesday, Dec. 27th, at 12 M. sharp. Band at 11.

J. B. WINSTON, } Managers.
EDWIN R. MACK, }

Emerson's Opera House,
San Francisco, Dec. 10th, 1878.
Protean Artist wanted. Would like to hear from Nina Saville.
12—1t*

Document No. 30.

Letter from Nina Saville to William Beauvoir.

NEW CENTREVILLE, December 26, 1878.

MY DEAR MR. BEAUVOIR:—I was very sorry to receive your letter of yesterday—*very* sorry—because there can be only one answer that I can make

—and you might well have spared me the pain of saying the word—No. You ask me if I love you. If I did—do you think it would be true love in me to tell you so, when I know what it would cost you? Oh indeed you must never marry *me!* In your own country you would never have heard of me—never seen me—surely never written me such a letter to tell me that you love me and want to marry me. It is not that I am ashamed of my business or of the folks around me, or ashamed that I am only the charity child of two poor players, who lived and died working for the bread for their mouths and mine. I am proud of them—yes, proud of what they did and suffered for one poorer than themselves—a little foundling out of an Indian camp. But I know the difference between you and me. You are a great man at home—you have never told me how great—but I know your father is a rich lord, and I suppose you are. It is not that I think *you* care for that, or think less of me because I was born different from you. I know how good—how kind—how *respectful* you have always been to me—*my lord*—and I shall never forget it—for a girl in my position knows well enough how you might have been otherwise. Oh believe me—*my true friend*—I am never going to forget all you have done for me—and how good it has been to have you near me—a man so different from most others—I don't mean only the kind things you have done—the books and the thoughts and the ways you have taught me to enjoy —and all the trouble you have taken to make me something better than the stupid little girl I was when you found me—but a great deal more than that—the consideration you have had for me and for what I hold best in the world.   I had never met a *gentleman* before—and now the first one I meet—he is my *friend*.   That is a great deal.   ·

Only think of it! You have been following me around now for three months, and I have been weak enough to allow it.   I am going to do the right thing now. You may think it hard in me *if you really mean what you say*, but even if everything else were right, I would not marry you—because of your rank.   I do not know how things are at your home —but something tells me it would be wrong and that your family would have a right to hate you and never forgive you.   Professionals cannot go in your society.   And that is even if I loved you—and I do not love you—I do not love you—*I do not love you* —now I have written it you will believe it.

So now it is ended—I am going back to the line I was first in—variety —and with a new name.   So

you can never find me—I entreat you—I beg of you
not to look for me. If you only put your mind
to it—you will find it so easy to forget me for I
will not do you the wrong to think that you did not
mean what you wrote in your letter or what you
said that night *when we sang Annie Laurie together*
the last time. Your sincere friend,

NINA.

Documents Nos. 31 and 32.

*Items from the San Francisco "Figaro" of December
29th, 1878.*

Nina Saville Co. disbanded New Centreville 26th.
No particulars received.

Winston & Mack's Comb. takes the road December 31st, opening at Tuolumne Hollow. Manager
Winston announces the engagement of Anna Laurie,
the Protean change artiste, with songs, "Don't Get
Weary," "Bobbin' Around," "I Yoost Landet."

Document No. 33.

*Telegram from Zeke Kilburn, New Centreville, to
Winston and Mack, Emerson's Opera House, San
Francisco, Cal.*

NEW CENTREVILLE, Dec. 28, 1878.

Have you vacancy for active and energetic advance agent.

Z. KILBURN.

(9 words 30 paid.)

Document No. 34.

Telegram from Winston and Mack, San Francisco, to Zeke Kilburn, New Centreville.

SAN FRANCISCO, Dec. 28, 1878.

No.

WINSTON & MACK.

(Collect 30 cents.)

Document No. 35.

Bill sent to William Beauvoir, United States Hotel, Tuolumne Hollow, Cal.

Tuolumne Hollow, Cal., Dec. 29, 1878.

William Beauvoir, Esq.

Bought of HIMMEL & HATCH,

Opera House Block,

JEWELLERS & DIAMOND MERCHANTS.

Dealers in all kinds of Fancy Goods, Stationery, and Umbrellas, Watches, Clocks, and Barometers.

TERMS CASH.   MUSICAL BOXES REPAIRED.

Dec. 29. *One diamond and enamelled locket,*	$75.00
One gold chain, ...	48.00
	$123.00

Rec'd Payt.

Himmel & Hatch,
per S.

V.

Document No. 36.

Letter from Cable J. Dexter, Esq., to Messrs. Pixley and Sutton, San Francisco.

NEW CENTREVILLE, March 3, 1879.

MESSRS. PIXLEY & SUTTON.

GENTS:—I am happy to report that I have at last reached the bottom level in the case of William Beaver, *alias* Beaver Bill, deceased through Indians in 1861.

In accordance with your instructions and check, I proceeded, on the 10th ult., to Shawgum Creek, where I interviewed Blue Horse, chief of the Comanches, who tomahawked subject of your inquiries in the year above mentioned. Found the Horse in the penitentiary, serving out a drunk and disorderly. Though belligerent at date aforesaid, Horse is now tame, though intemperate. Appeared unwilling to converse, and required stimulants to awaken his memory. Please find inclosed memo. of account for whiskey, covering extra demijohn to corrupt jailer. Horse finally stated that he personally let daylight through deceased, and is willing to guarantee thoroughness of decease. Stated further that aforesaid Beaver's family consisted of squaw and kid. Is willing to swear that squaw was killed, the tribe having no use for her. Killing done by Mule-Who-Goes-Crooked, personal friend of Horse's. The minor child was taken into camp and kept until December of 1863, when tribe dropped to howling cold winter and went on government reservation. Infant (female) was then turned over to U. S. Government at Fort Kearney.

I posted to last-named locality on the 18th ult., and found by the quartermaster's books that, no one appearing to claim the kid, she had been duly indentured, together with six Indians, to a man by the name of Guardine or Sardine (probably the latter), in the show business. The Indians were invoiced as Sage Brush Jimmy, Boiling Hurricane, Mule-Who-Goes-Crooked, Joe, Hairy Grasshopper, and Dead Polecat. Child known as White Kitten. Receipt for Indians was signed by Mr. Hi. Samuels, who is still in the circus business, and whom I happen to be selling out at this moment, at suit of McCullum & Montmorency, former partners. Samuels positively identified kid with variety specialist by name of Nina Saville, who has been showing all through this region for a year past.

I shall soon have the pleasure of laying before you documents to establish the complete chain of evidence, from knifing of original subject of your inquiries right up to date.

I have to-day returned from New Centreville, whither I went after Miss Saville. Found she had just skipped the town with a young Englishman by the name of Bovoir, who had been paying her polite attentions for some time, having bowied or otherwise squelched a man for her within a week or two. It appears the young woman had refused to have anything to do with him for a long period; but he seems to have struck pay gravel about two days before my arrival. At present, therefore, the trail is temporarily lost; but I expect to fetch the couple if they are anywhere this side of the Rockies.

Awaiting your further instructions, and cash backing thereto, I am, gents, very resp'y yours,

CABLE J. DEXTER.

Document No. 37.

Envelope of letter from Sir Oliver Beauvoir, Bart., to his son, William Beauvoir.

Sent to Dead Letter Office

William Beauvoir, Esq.
Sherman House Hotel
Chicago
United States of America

Not here
try Brevoort House
N. Y.

Document No. 38.

Letter contained in the envelope above.

CHELSWORTH, March 30, 1879.

MY DEAR BOY:—In the sudden blow which has come upon us all I cannot find words to write. You do not know what you have done. Your uncle William, after whom you were named, died in America. He left but one child, a daughter, the only grandchild of my father except you. And this daughter is the Miss Nina Saville with whom you have formed so unhappy a connection. She is your own cousin. She is a Beauvoir. She is of our blood, as good as any in England.

My feelings are overpowering. I am choked by the suddenness of this great grief. I cannot write to you as I would. But I can say this: Do not let me see you or hear from you until this stain be taken from our name.

OLIVER BEAUVOIR.

Document No. 39.

Cable dispatch from William Beauvoir, Windsor Hotel, New York, to Sir Oliver Beauvoir, Bart., Chelsworth, Suffolk, England.

NEW YORK, May 1, 1879

Have posted you *Herald.*

WILLIAM BEAUVOIR.

Document No. 40.

Advertisement, under the head of " Marriages" from the New York " Herald," April 30th, 1879.

BEAUVOIR—BEAUVOIR.—On Wednesday, Jan. 1st, 1879, at Steal Valley, California, by the Rev. Mr. Twells, William Beauvoir, only son of Sir Oliver Beauvoir, of Chelsworth, Suffolk, England, to Nina, only child of the late William Beauvoir, of New Centreville, Cal.

Document No. 41.

Extract from the New York " Herald" of May 29th, 1879.

Among the passengers on the outgoing Cunard steamer *Gallia*, which left New York on Wednesday, was the Honorable William Beauvoir, only son of Sir Oliver Beauvoir, Bart., of England. Mr. Beauvoir has been passing his honeymoon in this city, and, with his charming bride, a famous California belle, has been the recipient of many cordial courtesies from members of our best society. Mr. William Beauvoir is a young man of great promise and brilliant attainments, and is a highly desirable addition to the large and constantly increasing number of aristocratic Britons who seek for wives among

the lovely daughters of Columbia.   We understand
that the bridal pair will take up their residence with
the groom's father, at his stately country-seat, Chelsworth Manor, Suffolk.

SEVEN CONVERSATIONS

OF

DEAR JONES AND BABY VAN RENSSELAER,

(In Collaboration with H. C. Bunner.)

SEVEN CONVERSATIONS

OF

DEAR JONES AND BABY VAN RENSSELAER.

I.

THE FIRST CONVERSATION.

TUESDAY, February 14, 1882.

The band was invisible, but, unfortunately, not inaudible. It was in the butler's pantry, playing Waldteufel's latest waltz, "Süssen Veilchen." The English butler, who resented the intrusion of the German leader, was introducing an *obbligato* unforeseen by the composer. This was the second of Mrs. Martin's charming Tuesdays in February. Mrs. Martin herself, fondly and familiarly known as the "Duchess of Washington Square," stopped a young man as he was making a desperate rush for his overcoat, then reposing under three strata of late comers' outer garments in the second floor back, and said to him:

"O Dear Jones"—the Duchess always called him
Dear Jones—"I want to introduce you to Baby Van
Rensselaer—Phyllis Van Rensselaer, you know—
they always called her Baby Van Rensselaer, though
I'm sure I don't know why— Phyllis is such a lovely
name—don't you think so?—and your grandfathers
were such friends." [Dear Jones executed an *ex
post facto* condemnation upon his ancestor and hers.]
"You know Major Van Rensselaer was your grand-
father's partner until that unfortunate affair of the
embezzlement—O Baby dear—there you are, are
you? I was wondering where you were all this
time. This is Mr. Jones, dear, one of your grand-
father's most intimate friends. Oh, I don't mean
that, of course—you know what I mean--and I do
so want you two to know each other."

DEAR JONES: What in the name of the prophet
does the Duchess mean by introducing me to More
Girls?

BABY VAN RENSSELAER: I do wish the Duchess
wouldn't insist on tiring me out with slim young
men; I never can tell one from the other.

These remarks were not uttered. They remained in
the privacy of the inner consciousness. What
they really said was:

DEAR JONES [*inarticulately*]: Miss Van Rensselaer.

BABY VAN RENSSELAER [*inattentively*]: Yes, it *is* rather warm. . . .

And they drifted apart in the crowd.

II.

THE SECOND CONVERSATION.

THURSDAY, April 13, 1882.

Of course, Dear Jones was the last to arrive of the favored children of the world who had been invited to dine at Judge Gillespie's "to meet the Lord Bishop of Barset," just imported from England per steamer *Servia.* In the hall, the butler, whose appearance was even more dignified and clerical than the Bishop's, handed Dear Jones an unsealed communication.

DEAR JONES [*examining the contents*]: Who in Heligoland is Miss Van Rensselaer?

As Dear Jones entered, Mrs. Sutton—the Judge's daughter, you know—married Charley Sutton, who came from San Francisco—Mrs. Sutton gave a little sigh of relief, nodded to the butler, and said in perfunctory answer to the apologies Dear Jones had not made: "Oh, no; you're not a bit late—we haven't been waiting for you at all—the Bishop has only just come"—(confidentially in his ear) "I 've given you a charming girl." [Dear Jones shuddered: he knew what that generally meant.] "You know Baby Van Rensselaer? Of course—there she is—

now, go—and do be bright and clever." And after thus handicapping an inoffensive young man, she took the Bishop's arm in the middle of his ante-prandial anecdote.

DEAR JONES [*marching to his fate*]: It's the Duchess's girl again, by Jove! It's lucky Uncle Larry is going to take me off at ten sharp.

BABY VAN RENSSELAER: Why, it's *that* Mr. Jones!

These remarks were not uttered. They remained in the privacy of the inner consciousness. What they really said was:

DEAR JONES [*with audacious hypocrisy*]: Of course, *you* don't remember me, Miss Van Rensselaer. . . .

BABY VAN RENSSELAER [*trumping his card un-abashed*]: I really don't quite. . . .

DEAR JONES [*offering his arm*]: Er . . . don't you remember the Duch—Mrs. Martin's—that hideously rainy afternoon, just before Lent?

Here there was a gap in the conversation as the procession took up its line of march, and moved through a narrow passage into the dining-room.

DEAR JONES [*making a brave dash at the " bright and clever "*]: Well, in *my* house, the door into the dining-room shall be eighteen feet wide.

BABY VAN RENSSELAER [*literal, stern, and cold*]:
Are you building a house, Mr. Jones?

DEAR JONES [*calmly*]: I am at present, Miss Van
Rensselaer, building—let me see—four—five—seven
houses.

BABY VAN RENSSELAER [*coldly and suspecting flip-
pancy*]: Ah, indeed—are you a billionaire?

DEAR JONES: No; I'm an architect.

BABY VAN RENSSELAER [*in confusion*]: Oh, I'm
sure I beg your pardon——

DEAR JONES: You needn't. I shouldn't be at all
ashamed to be a billionaire.

BABY VAN RENSSELAER: Oh, of course not—I
didn't mean *that*——

DEAR JONES [*unguardedly*]: Well, if it comes to
that, I'm not ashamed of my architecture either.

BABY VAN RENSSELAER [*calmly*]: Indeed? I
have never seen any of it.

DEAR JONES: You sit here, I think. This is your
card with the little lady in the powdered wig—a
cherubic Madame de Staël.

BABY VAN RENSSELAER: And this is yours with
a Cupid in a basket—a nineteenth-century Moses.

DEAR JONES [*taking his seat beside her*]: Talking
about dinner cards—and billionaires, you heard of
that dinner old Creasers gave to fifty-two of his

friends of the new dispensation. I believe there *was* one poor fellow there whose wife had only half a deck of diamonds. He assembled his hordes in the picture-gallery, as the dining-room wasn't large enough —you see, I didn't build *his* house. And to carry out the novelty of the thing, his dinner cards were——

BABY VAN RENSSELAER: Playing-cards?

DEAR JONES: Just so—but they were painted, "hand-painted" on satin.

BABY VAN RENSSELAER: And what did he take for himself—the king of diamonds?

DEAR JONES: For the only time in his life he forgot himself—and he had to put up with the Joker.

BABY VAN RENSSELAER: What sort of people were there?

DEAR JONES: Very good sort, indeed. There was a M. Meissonier and a M. Gérôme and a M. Corot—besides the man who sold them to him.

Everybody knows how a conversation runs on at dinner, when it does run on. On this occasion it ran on for seventy minutes and six courses. Dear Jones and Baby Van Rensselaer discussed the usual topics and the usual bill of fare. Then, as the butler served the bombe *glacée à la Demidoff*—

BABY VAN RENSSELAER: Oh, I'm so glad you

liked her. We were at school together, you know, and she was with us when we went up the Saguenay last August.

DEAR JONES: Why, *I* went up the Saguenay last August.

BABY VAN RENSSELAER [*earnestly*]: And we didn't meet? How miserably absurd!

DEAR JONES: I'll tell you whom I did meet—your father's partner, Mr. Hitchcock. He had his daughter with him, too—a very bright girl. You know her, of course.

BABY VAN RENSSELAER [*coldly*]: I have heard she is quite clever. [*A pause.*] The Hitchcocks— I believe—go more in the—New England set. I have met her brother, though—Mr. Mather Hitchcock. . . .

DEAR JONES: Mat Hitchcock; that little cad?

BABY VAN RENSSELAER: Is he a little cad? I thought he was rather—bright.

After this, conversation was desultory; and soon the male guests were left to their untrammelled selves, tobacco, and the Bishop. At eleven minutes past ten, in the vestibule of Judge Gillespie's house, a young man and a man not so young were buttoning their overcoats and lighting their cigarettes. In the parlor behind them a soft contralto voice was lingering on the rich, deep notes of " Der Asra," the sweetest song of Jewish inspiration, the song of Heine and of Rubinstein. They paused a moment as the voice died away in

> " Und mein Stamm sind jene Asra,
> Welche sterben wenn sie lieben ! "

The man not so young said: " Well, come along. What are you waiting for? "

DEAR JONES: What the devil are you in such a hurry for, Uncle Larry? It looked abominably rude to leave those people in that way!

III.

THE THIRD CONVERSATION.

TUESDAY, May 30, 1882.

As the first band of the Decoration Day procession struck up " Marching through Georgia " and marched past Uncle Larry's house, a cheerfully expectant party filed out of the parlor windows upon the broad stone balcony, draped with the flag that had floated over the building for the four long years the day commemorated. Uncle Larry had secured the Duchess to matronize the annual gathering of young friends, the final friendly meeting before the flight out of town; and many of those who accepted him as the universal uncle had accepted also this invitation. Dear Jones and Baby Van Rensselaer were seated in the corner of the balcony that caught the southern sun, Baby Van Rensselaer in Uncle Larry's own study chair, while Dear Jones was comfortably and gracefully perched on the broad brown-stone railing of the balcony.

BABY VAN RENSSELAER : Now, *doesn't* that music make your heart leap?

DEAR JONES: M' yes.

BABY VAN RENSSELAER : You know I haven't the

least bit of sympathy with that affected talk about not being moved by these things, and thinking it vulgar and all that. I'm proud to say I love my country, and I do love to see my country's soldiers. Don't you?

DEAR JONES: M'—yes.

BABY VAN RENSSELAER: Of course, I can't really remember anything about the war, but I try to pretend to myself that I do remember when I was held up at the window to see the troops marching back from the grand review at Washington. [*Rather more softly.*] Mamma told me about it often before she died. And " Marching through Georgia " always makes the tears come to my eyes; don't it yours?

DEAR JONES: M'—yes.

BABY VAN RENSSELAER: "Yes!" How queerly you say that!

DEAR JONES [*grimly*]: I'm rather more inclined to cry when the band makes

"Stream and forest, hill and strand,
Reverberate with ' Dixie.' "

BABY VAN RENSSELAER [*coldly*]: I'm afraid, Mr. Jones, I do not understand you. And you appear to have a very peculiar feeling about these things.

DEAR JONES [*rather absently*]: Well, yes, it is rather a matter of feeling with me. Weak, I sup-

7

pose but the fact is, Miss Van Rensselaer, it just breaks me up to see all this. You know, the war hit me pretty hard. I lost my brother in hospital after Seven Pines—and then I lost my father, the best friend I ever had, at Gettysburg, on the hill, you know, when he was leading his regiment, and his men couldn't make him stay back. So, you see I wouldn't have come here at all to-day if—if——

BABY VAN RENSSELAER: O Mr. Jones, I'm *so sorry.*

DEAR JONES [*surprised*]: Sorry? Why?

BABY VAN RENSSELAER: I didn't quite understand you—but I do now. Why, you're taking off your hat. What is it? Oh, the battle-flags!

DEAR JONES: My father's regiment.

BABY VAN RENSSELAER [*to herself*]: I wonder if that is the regiment I saw coming back from Washington?

IV.

THE FOURTH CONVERSATION.

TUESDAY, August 22, 1882.

The train rattled hotly along on its sultry journey from one end of Long Island to the other, a journey the half of which it had nearly accomplished with much fuss and fret. Leaving his impediments of travel in the smoker, Dear Jones entered the forward end of the parlor car in search of an uncontaminated glass of water. As he set down the glass he glanced along the car, and his manner changed at once. He opened the door for an instant and threw on the down track his half-smoked cigarette; and then, smiling pleasantly, he walked firmly down the car, past a rustic bridal couple, and took a vacant seat just in front of Baby Van Rensselaer.

BABY VAN RENSSELAER: Why, Mr. Jones!

DEAR JONES: Why, Miss Van Rensselaer!

BABY VAN RENSSELAER: Who would have thought of seeing you here in this hot weather?

DEAR JONES: Can I have this seat or is it that I *mank* at the *convenances*—as the French say?

BABY VAN RENSSELAER: It's Uncle Larry's chair —he's gone back to talk to one of his vestrymen—he's taking me to Shelter Island.

DEAR JONES: Shelter Island? How long are you going to stay there?

BABY VAN RENSSELAER: And where are you going?

DEAR JONES: I'm going to Sag Harbor to build a house for one of my billionaires.

BABY VAN RENSSELAER: Sag Harbor? What an extraordinary place for a house.

DEAR JONES: Oh, that's nothing. Last year I had to build a house up in Chemung County.

BABY VAN RENSSELAER: Chemung?

DEAR JONES [*spelling it*]: C-h-e-m-u-n-g'—accent on the mung. You probably call it Cheémung, but it is really Sh'mung.

BABY VAN RENSSELAER: Where is it? and how do you get there?

DEAR JONES: By the *Chemung de fer*, of course.

BABY VAN RENSSELAER: O Mr. Jones.

DEAR JONES: You see, my mind is relaxed by the effort to build a house on the model of the one occupied by the old woman who lived in a shoe·and that variety of early English architecture is very wearing on the taste. What sort of a house is it you are going to at Shelter Island? And how long are you going to stay there?

BABY VAN RENSSELAER: Oh, it's a stupid, old-fashioned place. [*Pause.*] Do you think that bride is pretty? I have been watching them ever since we left New York. They have been to town on their wedding-trip.

DEAR JONES: She is ratherish pretty. And he's a shrewd fellow and likely to get on. I shouldn't wonder if he was the chief wire-puller of his "dees-trick."

BABY VAN RENSSELAER: A village Hampden?

DEAR JONES: Some day he'll withstand the little tyrant of the fields and lead a revolt against the garden-sass monopoly, and so sail into the legisla-ture. I fear the bride is destined to ruin her diges-tion in an Albany boarding-house, while the groom gives his days and nights to affairs of state.

Here the train slackened its speed as it approached a small station from which shrill notes of music arose.

BABY VAN RENSSELAER: Look, the bride is going to leave us.

DEAR JONES: He lives here, and the local fife and drum corps have come to welcome him home.

Dinna ye hear that strident "Hail to the Chief" they have just executed?

BABY VAN RENSSELAER: How proudly she looks up at him! I think the band ought to play something for her—but they are men, and they'll never think of it.

DEAR JONES: You cannot expect much tact from two fifes and a bass drum, but unless my ears deceive me they have greeted the bride with a well-meant attempt at "Home, Sweet Home."

BABY VAN RENSSELAER:

> "And each responsive soul has heard
>   That plaintive note's appealing.
> So deeply 'Home, Sweet Home' has stirred
>   The hidden founts of feeling."

DEAR JONES [*surprised*]: Why—how did you know that poem?

BABY VAN RENSSELAER: Oh, I heard somebody quote it last Decoration Day—I don't know who—it struck me as very pretty and I looked it up.

DEAR JONES [*pleased*]: Oh, I remember. It has always been a favorite of mine.

BABY VAN RENSSELAER [*coldly*]: Indeed?

DEAR JONES [*as the train starts again*]: Bride and groom, fife and drum, fade away from sight and hearing. I wonder if we shall ever think of them again?

BABY VAN RENSSELAER: I shall, I'm sure. She was so pretty. And, besides, the music was lively. I shan't have anything half as amusing as that at Shelter Island.

DEAR JONES: Don't you like it, then?

BABY VAN RENSSELAER: Oh, dear, no! I shall be glad to get away to my aunt's place at Watch Hill. It's very poky indeed at Shelter Island. [*Sighs.*] And to think that I shall have to spend just two weeks of primness and propriety there.

DEAR JONES: Just two weeks? Ah!

V.

THE FIFTH CONVERSATION.

TUESDAY, September 5, 1882.   (Afternoon.)

Although it is difficult to tell the length from the breadth of the small steamer that plies between Sag Harbor and New London, it is safe to assume that it was the bow that was pointing away from the Shelter Island dock as Baby Van Rensselaer stepped out of the cabin and Dear Jones walked up to her, lifting his hat with an expression of surprise on his face that might have been better, considering that he had rehearsed it a number of times since he left Sag Harbor.

BABY VAN RENSSELAER: Why, Mr. Jones!

DEAR JONES [*forgetting his lines, and improvising*]: How—how—odd we should meet again just here.   Funny, isn't it?

BABY VAN RENSSELAER: It is exceedingly humorous.

DEAR JONES: I did not tell you, did I—when I saw you on the train, you know—that I had to go to New London, after I'd finished my work at Sag Harbor?

BABY VAN RENSSELAER [*uncompromisingly*]: I

don't think you said anything about New London at all.

DEAR JONES: I probably said the Pequot House. It's the same thing, you know. I have to go to New London to inspect the Race Rock light-house—you've heard of the famous light-house at Race Rock, of course.

BABY VAN RENSSELAER: I don't think its fame has reached me.

DEAR JONES: It's a very curious structure, indeed. And, the fact is, one of my—my billionaires—wants a light house. He has an extraordinary notion of building a light-house near his place on the sea-shore—a light-house of his own. Odd idea, isn't it?

BABY VAN RENSSELAER: It is a very odd proceeding altogether, I should say.

DEAR JONES: I suppose you mean that *I* am a very odd proceeding. Well, I will confess, and throw myself on your mercy. I *did* hope to meet you—and the Duch—Mrs. Martin. After two weeks of the society of billionaires, I think I'm excusable. . . . [*A painful pause.*] And I *had* to go to Race Rock, so I got off a day earlier than I had meant to, by cutting one of the turrets out of my original plan—he didn't mind—there are eleven left—and and—will you forgive me?

BABY VAN RENSSELAER: Really, I have nothing to forgive, Mr. Jones. I've no doubt my aunt will be very glad to see you.

DEAR JONES: Ah—how *is* Mrs. Martin?

BABY VAN RENSSELAER: She is in the cabin. She is quite well at present; but she is always very nervous about sea-sickness, and she prefers to lie down. I must go in and sit with her.

DEAR JONES [*quickly*]: Indeed—I didn't know Mrs. Martin suffered from sea-sickness. She's crossed the ocean so many times, you know. How many is it?

BABY VAN RENSSELAER: Six, I think.

DEAR JONES: No; eight, isn't it? I'm almost sure it's eight.

BABY VAN RENSSELAER: Very possibly. But she is a great sufferer. I must go and see how she is.

DEAR JONES: Yes, we'll go. I want to see Mrs. Martin. One of the disadvantages of the summer season is that one can't see the Duchess at regular intervals to exchange gossip.

BABY VAN RENSSELAER: Well, if you have any confidential gossip for the Duchess, I will wait here until you come out. I want to get all the fresh air possible, if I have to sit in the cabin for the rest of the trip.

DEAR JONES [*asserting himself*]: Very well. I have the contents of four letters from Newport to pour into the Duchess's ear. You know I was staying at the Hitchcocks' for a fortnight before I went to Sag Harbor.

He went into the stuffy little cabin, where the Duchess was lying on a bench, in a wilderness of shawls. Baby Van Rensselaer waited a good half-hour, but heard no sound of returning footsteps from that gloomy cave. Finally she went in to investigate, and was told by the Duchess that "Dear Jones has gone after, or whatever you call it, to smoke a cigar." Baby Van Rensselaer made up her mind that under those circumstances she would go forward and read her book. She also made up her mind that Mr. Jones was extremely rude. His rudeness, she found, as she sat reading at the bow of the boat, really spoiled her book. She knew that she ought not to let such little things annoy her; but, then, it was a very stupid chapter, and the fresh sea breeze blew the pages back and forwards, and her veil would not stay over her hair, and she always had hated travelling, and it was so disagreeable to have people behave in that way—especially people —well, any people. Just here she turned her head, and saw Dear Jones advancing from the cabin with a bright and smiling face.

BABY VAN RENSSELAER [*about to rise*]: My aunt wants me, I suppose.

DEAR JONES: Not at all—not in the least—at present. I just came through the cabin—on tiptoe —and she was fast asleep. In fact, not to speak it profanely, she was—she was audible.

BABY VAN RENSSELAER: Oh!

DEAR JONES: I'm glad to see you're getting the benefit of the fresh air.

BABY VAN RENSSELAER: I was afraid of waking my aunt with the rustling of the leaves of my book, so I came out here.

DEAR JONES: I'm glad you did. It would be a shame for you to have to sit in that close cabin. That's the reason I didn't come back to you when I left Mrs. Martin. I played a pious fraud on you for the benefit of your health.

BABY VAN RENSSELAER: You were very considerate.

DEAR JONES [*enthusiastically*]: Oh, not at all.

BABY VAN RENSSELAER [*calmly*]: And if you'll excuse me, I'll finish my book. I can't read in the cabin.

Baby Van Rensselaer resumed her reading and

found the book improved a little. After a while she looked up and saw Dear Jones sitting on the rail, meekly twirling his thumbs.

BABY VAN RENSSELAER [*after an effort at silence*]: Don't be so ridiculously absurd. What are you doing there?

DEAR JONES: I'm waiting to be spoken to.

Baby Van Rensselaer smiled. The boat had just swung out of the jaws of the bay. Overhead was the full glory of a sky which made one believe that there never was such a thing as a cloud. And they sped along over the sea of water in a sea of light. Just then there came from the depths under the cabin the rise and fall of a measured, mocking melody, high and clear as the notes of a lark.

BABY VAN RENSSELAER: Why, that must be a bird whistling—only birds don't whistle "Amaryllis."

DEAR JONES: 'Tisn't a bird—it's an engineer.

BABY VAN RENSSELAER: An engineer?

DEAR JONES: A grimy engineer. Quite a pathetic story, too. Some of the Sag Harbor people took him up as a boy. He had a wonderful ear and an extraordinary tenor voice. They were going to make a Mario of him. They paid for his education in New York, and then sent him over to Paris to the Conservatory to be finished off. And he hadn't been there six weeks before he caught the regular Paris pleurisy—it's an *article de Paris*, you know, and lost his voice utterly and hopelessly.

BABY VAN RENSSELAER: Oh!

DEAR JONES: And so he had to come back and engineer for his living.

BABY VAN RENSSELAER: How very sad. Now I can scarcely bear to hear him whistle.

DEAR JONES [*to himself*]: Well, I didn't mean to produce that effect. [*To her.*] Oh, he doesn't mind it a bit. Hear him now.

The engineer was executing a series of brilliant vari-
    ations on the " Air du Roi Louis XIII.," melting
    by ingenious gradations into the " Babies on our
    Block."

DEAR JONES [*hastily*]: Race Rock lies over that way. You can't see it yet—but you will after a while.

BABY VAN RENSSELAER: Oh, then, there is a Race Rock ?

DEAR JONES: Why, certainly. . . .

With this starter, it may readily be understood that a man of Dear Jones's fecundity of intellect and fine imaginative powers was able to fill the greater part of the afternoon with fluent conversa-

tion. Two or three times Baby Van Rensselaer
made futile attempts to go into the cabin to see
how the Duchess was sleeping; but as many times
she forgot her errand. There was a fair breeze
blowing from the northeast, but the sea was smooth,
and the little boat scarcely rocked on the long, low
waves. It was getting toward four o'clock when
there was a sudden stoppage of the engineer's whistling and of the machinery of the boat. Baby Van
Rensselaer sent Dear Jones back to inquire into the
cause, for they were alone on the broad sea, with
only a tantalizing glimpse of New London harbor
stretching out welcoming arms of green, with the
Groton monument stuck like a huge clothes-pin on
the left arm. Dear Jones came back, trying hard to
look decently perturbed and gloomy, but with a
barbarian joy lighting up his bronzed features.

BABY VAN RENSSELAER: What is it?

DEAR JONES: The machinery is on a dead centre.
And the whistling engineer says that he'll have to
wait until he can get into port and hitch a horse to
the crank to start her off again.

BABY VAN RENSSELAER: But how are we to get
into port?

DEAR JONES: The whistling engineer further
says that we are now drifting toward Watch Hill.

BABY VAN RENSSELAER: That's just where we want to go.

DEAR JONES: Yes. [*An unholy toot from the steam whistle.*] And there he is signalling that yacht to take us off!

BABY VAN RENSSELAER: I must go to my aunt now.

DEAR JONES: Why—there's no hurry.

BABY VAN RENSSELAER: No, but she'll be so frightened—she'll think it's going to blow up or something.

Baby Van Rensselaer disappeared in the depths of the cabin. Dear Jones disconsolately walked the deck in solitary silence for five minutes. When Baby Van Rensselaer reappeared, his spirits rose.

BABY VAN RENSSELAER: My aunt is afraid you may have difficulty in reaching New London to-night. She wants me to ask you if you won't stay over-night at her place at Watch Hill?

DEAR JONES: Won't I? Well, I will—have much pleasure in accepting your aunt's invitation.

VI.

THE SIXTH CONVERSATION.

Tuesday, September 5, 1882. (Evening.)

A row of Japanese lanterns shed a Cathayan light along the little path leading from the Duchess's house on a rocky promontory to the little beach which nestled under its shoulder. The moon softly and judiciously lit up the baby breakers which in Long Island Sound imitate the surf of the outer sea. It threw eerie shadows behind the bath-houses, and fell with gentle radiance upon two dripping but shapely figures emerging from the water, where the other bathers were unwisely lingering.

Dear Jones: I think this is simply delightful. I really never got the perfect enjoyment of an evening swim before.

Baby Van Rensselaer: I am glad you enjoyed it.

Dear Jones: There is something so charming in this aristocratic seclusion, with the shouts and laughter of the vulgar herd just far enough off to be picturesque--if you can call a noise picturesque.

8

BABY VAN RENSSELAER [*coldly*]: I think this beach might be a little more private—it's shared in common by these three cottages.

DEAR JONES: But they seem to be very nice people here. And they all swim so well, it quite put me on my mettle. You are really a splendid swimmer, do you know it? And that girl I towed out to the buoy, who is she?

BABY VAN RENSSELAER [*explosively*]: Mr. Jones, this is positively insulting!

DEAR JONES: Wh—what—wh—why? I don't understand you.

BABY VAN RENSSELAER: To pretend that you don't know that Hitchcock woman!

DEAR JONES [*innocently*]: Was that Miss Hitchcock? I didn't recognize her.

BABY VAN RENSSELAER: If this is your idea of humor, Mr. Jones, it is simply offensive!

DEAR JONES: But, upon my soul, I didn't know the girl—nor she me!

BABY VAN RENSSELAER: You didn't know her? After you have been staying two weeks at her house at Newport?

DEAR JONES [*with something like dignity*]: I was staying at her father's house, Miss Van Rensselaer, and Miss Hitchcock was away on a visit.

BABY VAN RENSSELAER: Up the Saguenay, perhaps?

DEAR JONES: Very likely. Miss Hitchcock may have left a large part of the Saguenay unexplored for all I know. I was introduced to her party only half an hour before we got off the boat at Quebec.

BABY VAN RENSSELAER: Long enough, however, to discover that she was " bright."

DEAR JONES: Quite long enough, Miss Van Rensselaer. One may find out a great deal of another's character in half an hour.

There was a pause, which was filled by the strains of a Virginia reel, coming from one of the cottages high up on the bank, where an impromptu dance was just begun. The moonlight fell on Baby Van Rensselaer's little white teeth, set firmly between her parted lips. The pause was broken.

BABY VAN RENSSELAER: If you propose to descend to brutality of this sort, Mr. Jones, I think we need prolong neither the conversation—nor the acquaintance.

DEAR JONES [*honestly*]: No—you can't mean that —Miss Van Rensselaer—Baby——

BABY VAN RENSSELAER: What, sir! Your familiarity is—I can't stand familiarity from you! [*She clinches her little hands.*]

DEAR JONES: You have no right to treat me like this. If I am familiar it is because I love you—and you know it!

BABY VAN RENSSELAER: This is the first I have heard of it, sir. I trust it will be the last. Will you kindly permit me to pass, or must I——

DEAR JONES: You may go where you wish, Miss Van Rensselaer. No, come, this is ridiculous - -

BABY VAN RENSSELAER: Is it?

DEAR JONES: I mean it is foolish. Don't let us——

BABY VAN RENSSELAER: Don't let us see each other again!

VII.

THE SEVENTH CONVERSATION.

THURSDAY, February 14, 1884.

As the soft, low notes of the wedding-march from "Lohengrin" fell gently from the organ-loft over the entrance of Grace Church, the quartet of able-bodied ushers passed up the centre aisle and parted the white ribbons—a silken barrier which they had gallantly defended for an hour in a vain effort to keep the common herd of acquaintance separate from the chosen many of the family. Behind them came two pretty little girls, strewing the aisle with white flowers from their aprons. The four brides-maids, two abreast, passed up the aisle after the little girls, proud in their reflected glory. Then came the bride, leaning on Judge Gillespie's arm, and radiant with youth and beauty and happiness. As the procession drew near the chancel-rail, the groom came from the vestry and advanced to meet her, accompanied by his best man, Uncle Larry, who relieved him of his hat and overcoat, the which he would dexterously return to him when the happy

couple should leave the church man and wife.   And
in due time the Bishop asked, " Wilt thou have this
Woman to thy wedded wife ? "

DEAR JONES: I will.

The Bishop asked again, " Wilt thou have this
Man to thy wedded husband ?'

BABY VAN RENSSELAER: I will.

As they knelt at the altar the sun came out and fell
through the window, and the stained glass sifted
down on them the mingled hues of hope and of
faith and love; and the Bishop blessed them.

EDGED TOOLS,

(In Collaboration with Walter Herries Pollock.)

EDGED TOOLS.

A TALE IN TWO CHAPTERS.

CHAPTER I.

MONSIEUR BLITZINI'S FIRST PERFORMANCE.

THE season was at its height at the little town of Witherington, on the south coast of England; and the presence there of three German bands and of a troupe of Tyrolese zither players might be taken as evidence that the season at Witherington was unusually brilliant. At the Pavilion on the Pier —and what self-respecting seaside resort is now without its Pier and Pavilion?—companies of strolling performers followed one another in rapid succession, and with equal success. A wandering Variety Show had lingered for nearly a week, so attractive had been the latest war-song which the Only Macfarlane had bellowed lustily in response to three encores at every performance. The celebrated Campbell Comedy Company had given a round of the Legitimate Drama—an elastic term

as Mr. Campbell understood it, for it allowed Miss
Dora Dartmore (Mrs. Campbell) to appear as the
heroines of the 'Lady of Lyons,' 'East Lynne,' 'A
Happy Pair,' and 'The Little Detective.' After
a week of the Legitimate Drama the celebrated
Campbell Comedy Company had departed, and the
small boys of Witherington had torn down the vast
pictorial posters in which Mr. Campbell was repre-
sented as shaking hands with David Garrick, while
Shakespeare hovered above them, distributing an
impartial blessing. Now a new advertisement was
to be read by those who were willing to pause before the hoardings scattered here and there through-
out the town. This advertisement was peculiar
enough to deserve reproduction here in full:

PAVILION HALL.

SEANCE PRESTIGISPIRITISTE.
BY
MONSIEUR BLITZINI.

This world-renowned *artiste* will visit Witherington and
perform at the Pavilion Hall at 8 P.M. on the evenings of
Friday and Saturday, August 13th and 14th, 1886.

IMPORTANT TO THOSE INTERESTED IN THE OCCULT!

NO MAHATMAS OR ESOTERIC BAMBOOZLING!!

READ A PLAIN TALE.

Monsieur Blitzini, far-famed as a professor of the so-called
Art of Magic, undertook, in the exercise of his calling, to

expose the tricks and fallacies of the Spiritualists (including
the Davenport Cabinet, the Light and Dark Séance, Material-
ization, etc., etc.). This he did with ease ; but in the course
of the experiments suggested by his researches, he, strange
to relate, made the singular and startling discovery that there
is, in very truth, a Sphere of Spirits or Genii with whom it
is possible for the duly initiated to enter into converse ; and,
pushing his investigations still further, he became possessed
of the extraordinary and wondrous powers which he will
have the honor of exhibiting.

Monsieur Blitzini used to perform his Marvels of Magic
by sleight of hand alone, the aid of profuse machinery being
in his opinion contemptible. Still stranger wonders he now
performs without any aid save that of the invisibles above
alluded to.

COME AND SEE.

At the end of the performance Monsieur Blitzini will be
happy to give a detailed account of his experiences and dis-
coveries to any intelligent member of the audience desiring
the same.

MONSIEUR BLITZINI,

PRESTIGISPIRITISTE,

PAVILION HALL, WITHERINGTON, AUGUST 13TH AND 14TH, AT
EIGHT PRECISELY.

One of these alluring advertisements was affixed
to the wall of the Pier Pavilion, but it did not at-
tract as much attention during the afternoon preceding Monsieur Blitzini's promised first performance as it deserved, for a band was playing in the
middle of the Pavilion, and at the end of the Pier
the noted Man Otter and his seven sons and daugh-

ters were giving their astonishing Aquatic Entertainment.

Monsieur Blitzini's advertisement had, however,
considerable interest for two men lounging along
the pier—two men whom a boy would have called
elderly, and whom an old man would have declared
young. They were Steele Wyoming, an American, and Cecil Cameron, an Englishman. They
paused before the placard and read it silently and
with profound absorption. A smile or two flitted
across the Englishman's face during the perusal,
but the humorous gloom of the American deepened.

"Cecil," said the latter solemnly, "this is tall
talk, but I like it."

"Steele," replied his friend, "I think it is more
fun than a barrel of monkeys."

"It is very strange," Wyoming remarked with
the air of a person making a serious confidence to
himself, "how well he can talk American. Much
better than I do, in fact."

"I had the advantage of studying it as a foreign
language," Cameron retorted with equal gravity.

"Perhaps that may be the true explanation,"
said the American. "Now what about this hanky
man?"

"I think he's just lovely," interrupted the Englishman. "The Esoteric touch is good, and so is the 'so-called Art of Magic.'"

"The contempt for 'the use of profuse machinery' is quite Machiavellian. Altogether he seems to have got hold of an idea both new and good. We've had over and over again the converted and unconverted and re-re-re-converted Spiritualist, but to happen on a new kind of spirits while you were engaged in exposing the bogus one is a good act."

"It's not half bad," Cameron added; "and I'm really grateful to him for saying nothing about that detestable rubbish, Thought-Reading. It would have been so easy for him to ring in the old Second-Sight business and to call it Thought-Reading by Spirits of the nth Sphere."

"Blitzini has a soul above that."

"We're going to see him?" asked Cameron.

Wyoming stared at him silently for a few seconds, and then said, "Why persist in asking foolish questions? As if any two members of the Rosicrucian Brotherhood could be anywhere and see an ad. of a fakir's show and keep away."

"That's so," said the Englishman, as they walked away.

Before they reached the end of the pier Cameron

paused suddenly, and grasped his companion's arm and said, " I've an idea ! "

" Then I would suggest that you freeze to it," remarked Wyoming, pleasantly.

" Sir," replied Cameron, " to speak your benighted tongue—I have no use for you. Yet I will relent and tell you my idea."

" Fire away ! "

" I will be brief. This Blitzini used to be a con-jurer, but now he pretends that he is a conjurer no more, as the newly-discovered spirits work all his tricks for him. This, naturally, is all jimmy, and he does his little deceptions just like any other conjurer, of course."

"Of course," Wyoming said, as Cameron drew breath.

" Now this is my idea. Suppose that there are really spirits of the nth sphere, and suppose that they are of a sensitive nature and do not like to be spoken of lightly——"

" The Huffy Spook," commented Wyoming, gravely, " isn't a bad notion."

" Spook, for all it is German, is a blessed word," said Cameron; " it is so much more expressive than ghost or spectre. But you do not yet catch on. Just imagine those spirits reading this advertisement and seeing themselves billed to perform out of their proper sphere. It seems to me that this placard is calculated to hold them up to ridicule and contempt among the spirits of other spheres."

"I see," Wyoming interrupted; "and I think they would be justified in getting mad."

"And wouldn't they be likely to go for that magician," asked Cameron, "and have some fun with him?"

"It would be a cold day for the unlucky fakir," assented Wyoming.

"I don't like to think what might happen," the Englishman continued.

The American smiled solemnly and said, "Well, with a bewildered and baffled conjurer and a lot of angry spooks lying around loose with their dander up, almost anything might happen. And, if anything should happen, why, as Artemus Ward says, it would be money in that man's pocket if he had never been born."

"Fancy, now," said Cameron; "what if this should occur to-night? He is to give his show for two evenings only. Do you know what to-day is?"

"Friday."

"Hangman's day, you know," Cameron continued, "and it's the thirteenth of the month."

"That's a curiously unlucky combination, isn't it?" the American asked. "I've had a baker's dozen of misfortunes happen to me on a Friday when it was a thirteenth. I guess we had better go to-night—perhaps something will happen."

"Meanwhile," said the Englishman, as they walked from the Pier upon the Esplanade, "we must dine. I want a square meal to give me strength to see the show. It's hot and dusty, so let's take a fly to the hotel—let's be hauled mealers, as you Americans say."

"It is wonderful," Wyoming remarked, as he beckoned to a cabman, "quite wonderful how well he speaks American."

"I learnt it," replied Cameron, with amazing effrontery, "from Henry James's novels."

After their dinner the two friends lighted their cigarettes and strolled slowly along the Esplanade to the Pier. When they reached the Pavilion they found a stream of spectators trickling into the hall where Monsieur Blitzini was to perform. At the suggestion of the American they tossed half a crown to see who should pay for the tickets. Wyoming lost, and he selected seats in the front row.

The hall was about half-full when they entered

it, and a few betarded stragglers came in while the
pianist was playing the overture.

"I know· this hall very well," said Cameron, as
they sat down; "I acted here last year in private
theatricals. It has one disadvantage, there is no
stage-door.· We had to come in at the main entrance just as we did to-night, and walk through
the auditorium to that door over there on the right
which leads to the stage and to the two dressing-
rooms alongside of it. We gave a comic opera,
and we were very cramped for space."

"I guess there will be room enough for the
spooks to put in their fine work," Wyoming answered, intensifying his Americanisms as he was
wont to do for the benefit of his English friend.

"Guess, spook, fine work. I'll get 'em all three
all ready," said Cameron, quoting Sir Andrew
Aguecheek. "Yours is a great language; though,
as I remarked before, you do draw on the German."

"I wonder what may be Monsieur Blitzini's native tongue?" asked Wyoming.

"*Monsieur* is French," answered Cameron, "*Blitz*
is German, and *ini* is Italian——"

"Then he is either an Irishman or a Russian,"
the American declared with an air of profound
wisdom.

9

"His programme is in French," Cameron re-marked as he bought one from the attendant; "at least it is in what purports to be French."

"It's a little short, isn't it?" the American que-ried; "seven tricks in the first part and six in the second."

"Total, thirteen again!" cried the Englishman.

At this moment the musician left off playing, and the curtain rose revealing a stage almost bare. There was an ordinary drawing-room table in the centre, and at the sides there were two smaller tables with glass tops; at the back there was a tall cone, like an extinguisher, except that it was quite seven feet high. Three or four of the footlights in the middle had been removed, and an inclined plane led from the stage about half-way down the centre of the hall. It was next to this "run-down," as it is technically called, that Cameron and Wyoming had taken their seats.

A few seconds after the curtain rose, Monsieur Blitzini appeared at the right of the stage, and ad-vancing to the centre he bowed to the audience. He was a man of less than forty. He was tall and slight, with a little stoop of the head. He had thick dark hair, already grizzled. He had a young-ish face, but it was heavily wrinkled. Heavy eyebrows arched over eyes which were his chief personal peculiarity; they were gray with a streak of red in the iris. His hands were fine and delicate, but there was a feline suggestion in their movements. The ease of his manner was not artificial, but it might fairly be called excessive.

"Ladies and gentlemen," he said, as he surveyed the audience calmly, "I hope to have the pleasure this evening of entertaining you with the sight of strange wonders. What I shall perform before you is so unlike the ordinary performance of the ordinary conjurer that without seeming boastful it would be impossible for me to expatiate on the extraordinary novelty of my programme, were it not that I cannot claim for myself any credit for the marvels which will be accomplished this evening. All that I have done is to discover the Spirits of the Silent Sphere and to induce them to lend us their aid for the working of many wonders. If, therefore, what you may see here to-night pleases you, it is these Spirits whom you must thank, not me. I am only a humble instrument in their hands, and they are the real authors of all the startling novelties which I hope to be able to exhibit before you this evening. I have to beg that you will bear this in mind. I use neither apparatus nor sleight-of-hand, nor do I rely in any way on my own dexterity or ingenuity. All that I do is to serve as the medium whereby these Spirits work wonders, closely akin to those which the Egyptian magicians wrought before Pharaoh—perhaps by the same means."

As Monsieur Blitzini finished this very irregular .speech, almost exactly the opposite of that ordinarily spoken by the professional conjurer, Cameron and Wyoming looked at each other in blank surprise.

"This is pretty steep, isn't it?" asked the American.

"It is that," the Englishman answered; "and I think it is about the coolest thing I ever heard. Just look over the programme, and you can recognize every trick on it, in spite of the fancy French names."

"*Le Bouquet d'Iris*," said Wyoming, "that's the growth of flowers, I suppose, and *La Pluie de Danaë* is the shower of money, of course. But what is *Le Tireur des Cartes?*"

"It's bad French for the rising cards, I'll be bound," Cameron answered. "And the others are all as familiar as these."

"You think, then, that he is hiding the old-fashioned tricks under new-fangled names, and that he is merely an ordinary conjurer, who has chosen to give variety to his show by alleging that familiar spirits come from the vasty deep to do his bidding?"

"Precisely so."

"It's a dodge worthy of Barnum at his best or Sarah Bernhardt," said the American, enthusiastically.

While the two friends were exchanging impressions Monsieur Blitzini had retired up the stage, as though to see that everything was in order. From the centre-table he had taken up his wand. With this in his right hand he advanced again to the foot-lights.

"I beg you will pardon this delay of a moment only, but you must observe that I have dispensed with an assistant, and that I shall not leave the stage during the performance. I shall remain before you the whole evening, except during the brief intermission between the two parts of the entertainment, and I shall have no assistance whatever— save the unseen hands of the Silent Spirits."

As he paused for a moment, Cameron said to Wyoming:

"He has a curious accent, hasn't he? It might be foreign—Dutch or Russian—and it might be English."

"He's not an American," replied Wyoming; "I feel sure of that."

'I shall have the pleasure of beginning my entertainment," Monsieur Blitzini continued, "with the strange marvel which I have called *Le Bouquet d'Iris.* I have here a flower-pot filled with garden-mould, and I take six seeds from this package, and ——" Here he interrupted himself and glanced with apparent surprise at the right lapel of his coat. "I beg your pardon, but I see I have presented myself before you without the flower which ought to adorn my button-hole. Now, I agree with a friend of mine who said he would rather wear a flower without a dress-coat than a dress-coat without a flower. Fortunately the omission is easily rectified. I take one of these seeds and I place it in my button-hole; I beg that the attendant spirits shall cause it to grow at once into a flower; I raise my wand in the air; I apply it to the button-hole; and you see——."

Monsieur Blitzini suited the action to the word, and the spectators did see. The seed in the button-hole grew at once to a large sunflower which spread over the lapel of his coat. Then suddenly its outer circle began to revolve and to crackle, while from the centre there shot out, with a sharp report, a long jet of flame. The sunflower had changed to a small Catherine wheel, which whirled round, banging, and blazing, and whizzing, and crackling until it had spent its short-lived fury. Monsieur Blitzini stood motionless in the centre of the stage, not lifting a finger to save his beard, which was getting singed, as the King of Spain's was by Drake. A look of surprise came into his gray eyes, and their red pupils glowed above the more material fireworks. At last the spinning wheel of fire gave a final blaze and a sudden bang, and died out and disappeared.

" I say," said Cameron, " this is something like a trick."

" As you justly observe," Wyoming returned, " it grows interesting. Who would have thought that the old flower trick had so much flame in it ? "

" A man must know his Shakespeare monstrous well to talk with you," Cameron answered.

" You see I'm an American," Wyoming replied, " and it is meat and drink to us to quote Shakespeare, even when we see a conjurer bound upon a wheel of fire, like King Lear. Did you notice that Blitzini seems quite as much surprised as we are ? "

" He bears the ordeal by fire very bravely," Cameron assented, " but I confess that I don't exactly understand this."

Meanwhile the spectators had been tumultuous

in their applause of this truly brilliant trick.   Monsieur Blitzini stood silent in the centre of the stage, bowing his acknowledgments, without a trace of the flower or of the fire which had followed it in the lapel of his coat.   His black doeskin coat was immaculate.   There was a flickering smile on his lips, and it seemed as though it was only by a strong effort that he was able to keep the wand in his hand from trembling.   As the applause died away he roused himself, and, taking up the flower pot, he descended the run-down and stood among the audience.   Here he finished the trick in more conventional fashion.   He borrowed a hat and held it over the flower-pot, and asked a lady to place her hands on the hat, and then removed the hat to reveal a beautiful bouquet of hot-house flowers standing upright in the earth of the pot.   He presented the bouquet to the lady gracefully, and then returned to the stage to bow again.

It was with a lighter heart, evidently, that he began the second trick on the programme, where it figured as *La Montre Indestructible*.   Under this title Monsieur Blitzini began to perform the familiar feat with a borrowed watch, which is first proved to be a repeater with the eccentric faculty of striking any hour that the owner may choose, and is then smashed to fragments in a mighty mortar. In the beginning of this trick, while the performer was among the audience, all went well; but at the end, when he returned to the stage and wrapped the shattered fragments in a sheet of paper, this sheet of paper suddenly disappeared, and the wheels and springs fell scattered on the stage. Wyoming noticed a curious and enigmatic expression in the conjurer's face as he stooped to gather up the broken bits. Monsieur Blitzini took another sheet of paper; and again it vanished from his fingers and again the fragments of the watch fell on the stage. Collecting them once more and taking a third sheet of paper, Monsieur Blitzini stepped out upon the run-down, and this time he was successful in making a parcel. He gave this parcel to the owner of the watch and asked him to open it, whereupon the time-piece was found intact.

"I shall now have the honor of showing you," said Monsieur Blitzini, as he again took up his position in the centre of the stage, "if the assistance I count upon from the Spirits of the Silent Sphere is vouchsafed to me, the wondrous experiment which I have called *L'Ecole de Cuisine tenue par Belialides.*"

"His French accent is good," Cameron remarked.

"But he isn't easy in his mind," answered Wyoming, who kept his eyes fixed on the face of the magician.

"I shall now," continued Monsieur Blitzini, "venture to tax your good-nature again by requesting the loan of a hat." As he came down from the stage his eye caught that of Wyoming, to whose questioning look he returned a glance of reassurance. Cameron and his friend had seen already that the performer had recognized them as experts in the art; and they were conscious that, as is the custom of conjurers, he was playing at them. Wyoming held up his hat, and the magician smilingly took it from him and returned to the stage.

L'École de Cuisine tenue par Belialides was soon seen to be a variation on the familiar trick of the omelette cooked in the hat over the flame of a candle—the trick over which Robert Houdin, in his 'prentice days, burnt his fingers and the borrowed hat. Monsieur Blitzini broke an egg into Wyoming's hat, whereat the young ladies in the audience giggled convulsively. He added butter and salt and pepper, and he stirred these together furiously with a long-handled spoon—such as a man should have when he sups with the devil. Then he held the hat over a candle, and a sudden smoke arose,

and a fragrant odor was wafted across the footlights.
It was clearly evident that the trick had been accomplished. Monsieur Blitzini laid the hat on the
stage just in front of the run-down, and was about
to put his hand into it to withdraw the omelette,
chatting pleasantly the while and making many
small jokes about his own culinary facilities, when
he happened to cast his eyes into the hat. Instantly
he withdrew his hand, and started back in undis
guised astonishment commingled with terror. The
head of a large snake protruded from the hat and
extended itself threateningly. With a sinuous
movement it thrust itself forward from the hat and
started toward the spectators. It was a huge boa-
constrictor, apparently, and in girth it was almost
equal to the hat from which it was proceeding. The
magician stood stock-still on one side, staring at
the serpent as though fascinated; only a tremor in .
his knees betrayed his fear. The head of the great
snake crossed the two yards or more of the space
between the hat and the footlights, and still the
body continued to emerge from the hat. At last
it arrived at the run-down, and with a slight effort
it raised itself and started to cross this little bridge
to reach the audience. There was a sudden movement of alarm among the spectators, most of whom

thought that the appearance of the serpent was part of the trick, and were yet frightened by the fearful reality; but this alarm was allayed when the head of the snake, as it entered on the run-down and passed the line of the footlights, suddenly vanished. The tortuous body could be seen rising from the hat and pressing forward only to become invisible as it left the stage. It was some seconds after the head had disappeared before the tail of the snake left the hat, but soon it followed the headless body, which continued to move toward the spectators and which was steadily disappearing as it left the stage. The tail advanced nearer the line of the footlights until only a yard of the snake's length was to be seen. then only half a yard was visible; at last the final few inches, thin and tapering, passed across the diminishing distance, until, with a sinister vibration, the tip of the tale waved itself upon the run-down and into invisible space.

Cameron and Wyoming looked at each other for a moment, and then turned again to watch Monsieur Blitzini, from whom they had hardly taken their eyes during the brief minute of the huge serpent's existence. They saw him give one gasp before he recovered himself sufficiently to take the abundant applause which followed an effect as novel and as surprising and as inexplicable as this. He snatched up the hat from the floor and rushed upon the run-down. Then he paused and drew a long breath. In a moment he had turned out upon a plate, with which he had previously provided one of the spectators, the smoking omelette of which the appetizing odors had been perceived before the appearing of the snake, and he had returned the hat unimpaired to Wyoming.

"He works neatly," said Cameron.

"But he is powerful scared," Wyoming answered. "These new variations on the old tricks surprise him as much as they do us."

"Perhaps our joke is coming true—the spirits have taken umbrage at his unauthorized use of their names, and they are playing tricks on him."

"Do you think that his familiar spook has gone back on him?" asked Wyoming.

"What else can I think?" returned Cameron. "The Huffy Spook theory is the only tenable one."

"It will serve as a working hypothesis at least," Wyoming assented. "But why is it that all goes well while he is down here among the audience, and that everything goes wrong when he is up there on the stage? Have you noticed it?"

"Yes," Cameron answered, "I see it, and it is queer."

Of the next two items on the programme there is no need to speak in detail. The tricks were commonplace enough in themselves, but they proved to be quite uncommon in their execution. There was nothing as surprising or as startling as the serpent which rose from the hat and disappeared by inches with a sharp line as though it had been cut off with a knife, but they were astonishing enough.

Wyoming kept close watch of the magician's face, and he noted all his movements, and he saw that Monsieur Blitzini, in so far as possible, kept among the spectators and away from the stage. He was confirmed in his idea that it was only on the further side of the footlights that the indignant spirits were able to take advantage of the conjurer's weakness. Monsieur Blitzini had full control of his resources so long as he was in the midst of the audience, and both tricks went well enough until the exigencies of the performance forced the magician to return to the stage.

And so it was with the sixth trick on the programme, which was called *Le Tireur des Cartes*, but which Wyoming and Cameron soon recognized as the familiar illusion known as the Rising Cards, and justly popular among all modern magicians, as it is almost the only card-trick which is showy enough for a large hall.

Monsieur Blitzini took a pack of cards in his hand, came down among the audience, and performed a series of most ingenious sleights. He passed cards into a man's pocket and he drew cards from a lady's fan. He gave one spectator a black card to hold, and then touched it with his wand, and, lo! it was a red card. He bade another spectator think of a card, and he then asked him if he would prefer to find it at the top or the bottom of the pack, and when the spectator chose the top, he turned over the uppermost card and it was the one thought of. At last he asked six different persons in different parts of the hall to draw cards and return them to the pack, which, when this had been done, was thoroughly shuffled. ⋅

Monsieur Blitzini went back to the stage and placed the pack in a glass goblet, and with this in his hand he advanced towards the footlights. Turning to the spectator who had drawn the first of the six cards, he said, " Will you please ask your card to rise from the pack ? "

Before the spectator could make this request a card jumped from the pack, flew to the side of the stage, and fixed itself to the scene.

Monsieur Blitzini's voice quavered as he asked: " Is that your card, sir ? "

" No," was the uncompromising answer.

A second card rose from the pack, skimmed through the air, and fastened itself on the scene on the other side of the stage.

" Is that your card ? " asked Monsieur Blitzini doubtfully.

" No," answered the spectator again.

A third card, a fourth, and a fifth rose from the pack in rapid succession, danced about the stage, and affixed themselves here and there on the scenery. They were followed by a dozen more, which rose in a bunch, flew separately through the air, and attached themselves to every salient object on the stage.

" Do you see your card, sir ? " Monsieur Blitzini inquired again, with an obvious uneasiness in his tone.

And again the spectator answered:

" No."

Monsieur Blitzini had come near the footlights to ask this question, and he now stepped out upon the run-down with the glass containing the remaining cards in his right.hand.

"What was your card?" he asked with a disheartened smile.

"The king of diamonds," the spectator replied; and as he spoke the king of diamonds rose from the pack and bowed gracefully.

The spell of ill luck was broken, and the five other cards rose in turn from the pack. Monsieur Blitzini was again able to bow acknowledgments to the round of applause which always greets this favorite feat when it is properly performed. Wyoming, who was a close observer—he was an excellent poker-player—noticed that although the magician's lips smiled, his eyes did not.

The final number of the first part of the programme purported to be *La Pluie de Danaë*, which Wyoming and Cameron had guessed to be a fantastic title for the familiar and effective trick generally known as the Shower of Money. In this surmise they were right. With admirable dexterity Monsieur Blitzini seemed to catch sovereigns out of the circumambient air; he found them in the bonnets of the ladies and in the beards of the men; he discovered them here, there, and everywhere; he borrowed a hat, and he threw into it enough gold

10

apparently to suffice to fill it to the brim.   He gave
a pretty touch to the trick by making an ever-in-
creasing arc of gold pieces stretch from one hand
to the other, and then from one hand into the hat—
"like a bar-tender mixing drinks and pouring a
cocktail from a glass in his right hand to a glass in
his left," as Wyoming described it.

While performing this ingenious variation on an
old trick, Monsieur Blitzini backed slowly up the
run-down, with the shower of gold apparently increasing in volume.   From a hasty glance he cast
behind him, Cameron and Wyoming guessed that
he meant to carry the trick right back to the extreme limit of the shallow stage.   Suddenly something happened which delighted the rest of the
spectators, although it caused the two friends a
painful surprise.

Monsieur Blitzini had scarcely more than set his
foot on the stage, with the shower of gold still fall-
ing, when the sovereigns disappeared, and in their
place appeared a host of short stout cudgels, which
began to descend in a rain of pelting blows on the
conjurer's back and shoulders and arms.   This
spectacle of a man taken at a physical disadvantage
caused the audience the greatest possible delight.
Even the more knowing ones, who felt sure that it

was part of the trick, applauded the scared look and pained expression which crossed Monsieur Blitzini's face, and which they accepted as the perfection of acting.

" The spooks are playing it pretty low down on the wonder-worker, it seems to me," said Wyoming compassionately.

" A stuffed club is no joke," Cameron answered.

Monsieur Blitzini's weird face had undergone many changes of expression since the sudden trans-mutation of the precious metal to dull wood. Amazement, pain, terror, and despair chased each other across his features. Unable at last to bear the unexpected visitation any longer, the magician fled headlong to the run-down. As he crossed the line of the footlights, the shower of bludgeons vanished utterly, and an arc of sovereigns began again, fall ing from his hand to the hat. He closed this into the hat, showed that the hat was absolutely empty, and then returned it to its owner as swiftly as he could.

He stood before the spectators perturbed and panting, and he bowed again and again before the plaudits of the audience, getting his breath back in the brief respite to announce that this concluded the first part of the entertainment, and that there would be an intermission of ten minutes. With another salutation he withdrew, returning to the stage and walking off hastily to the right.

"Well," said Wyoming, as the magician disap-peared from view, "what do you think now?"

"I don't know what to think, as I said before. It's a very picturesque performance, I take it, all round."

"I think I've found out the secret.'

"Stand and deliver," said Cameron.

"Assuming that these disturbances are caused by exasperated spirits, as we are justified in doing   "

"Of course we are," interrupted Cameron; "you and I know modern magic from Alfred to Omaha, and we know that these little effects are quite be-yond this man's power to control."

"Assuming this, I say," Wyoming continued, "we have to discover why it is that Monsieur Blitzini meets with no misadventures except when he is on the stage. Now I have a theory. The front of the stage is circular, and it is only behind the arc of the footlights that the spirits torment him. It has struck me that perhaps there has been a reversal of the sacred circle of fire within which the sorcerer who evoked spirits was safe from their assaults."

"A circle such as Benvenuto Cellini drew about him when he spent a lively night with the spooks in the Coliseum at Rome—is that what you mean?"

"Precisely," answered Wyoming. "He was safe within the mystic ring of flame because the spirits were without and could not break in. But Blitzini is at the mercy of the spirits confined within the flaming segment of the footlights, and he is only free from torment and torture when he breaks out."

"I shouldn't wonder if you were right," Cameron remarked, after a moment's thought. "Your theory that he is the slave of the lamps and of the ring at least explains the phenomenon, which is otherwise almost inexplicable."

During the performance of the second part of Monsieur Blitzini's programme the two friends had many opportunities of verifying the hypothesis, and they found that it was in accord with the facts. One of the tricks was performed wholly among the spectators without the return of the magician to the stage, and in this Monsieur Blitzini was perfectly successful and no untoward incident marked its performance. But the very next illusion, called *La Boisson de Tantale*, required the constant presence of the conjurer on the stage, where he operated an exchange of two liquors, filling two decanters placed at opposite extremities of the footlights; and although the ignorant spectators saw nothing at all unusual in the substitution of a cone of blue fire for a bottle of brandy, Wyoming and Cameron knew that the mocking spirits were again taking a freakish revenge on the froward magician who had dared to use their names without asking their permission In another trick, which appeared on the bills as *Les Drapeaux de l'Univers*, and which required the conjurer to produce mysteriously a bundle of the flags of all nations, the spirits again gained the upper hand and changed the pretty silken emblems into a stiff cactus, the sharp branches of which bristled with thorns In desperation Monsieur Blitzini crossed the line of the footlights, his face white with apprehension, but a glance of rigid determination still gleaming from his eye; no sooner had he stepped out upon the run-down than the green cactus gave way to a sheaf of Italian flags. In yet another illusion, the next to the last, entitled *Un Duel aux Cartes*, a card chosen by one of the audience was to be caught on the point of a sword when the spectator threw the pack in the air. The preliminary flourishes of the trick performed amid the audience were accomplished without let or hindrance, but when Monsieur Blitzini took up his po-

sition in the centre of the stage with the naked sword
in his right hand, and when the spectator threw the
cards towards him, the blade changed suddenly into
a revolver, and the pack was riddled by six bullets
discharged by the magician involuntarily, and as
though in obedience to a will stronger than his own.

"That is pretty good. I wonder what he will do
next," said Cameron, quoting the charming tale of
the parrot and the exploded ship.

"If he has as much sense as I give him credit for,"
replied Wyoming, "he will crawl along to the last
trick like a streak of greased lightning."

Cameron referred to his programme, "*Le Mage
Invisiblique* is the last trick."

"*Invisiblique* is good," Wyoming remarked. "I'd
like to know what it means."

"I take it to imply either that the *mage*—that is
Monsieur Blitzini himself, of course—becomes in
visible, or that he has his eyes blindfolded so that
he cannot see. We've paid our money, and he will
take his choice."

"I have been wondering what he means to do
with that tall cone there at the back. He must use
it in this trick somehow," Wyoming said; "it looks
like a huge extinguisher, doesn't it?—fit to put out
the candles of Giant Blunderbore."

As the American spoke, Monsieur Blitzini brought the cone forward and placed it by the side of one of the light little round tables, of which there were two, one at the right and one at the left of the stage. To the sharp eyes of the two friends it was evident that the magician's nerves were unstrung, and that he was in great haste to get to the end of his programme. He darted now and again suspicious glances behind him, as though in trepidation and bodily fear. When he began to speak his voice was flurried and broken.

"Time runs short," said Monsieur Blitzini, facing the audience, "and I am now approaching the conclusion of my entertainment. I do not like to tax the kindness or to impose on the patience of my friends, the Spirits of the Silent Sphere"—and here he shuddered slightly—"by whose aid I have been enabled to work the wonders you have beheld this evening. I shall have the honor of concluding my entertainment by exhibiting before you the strange feat which I have called the *Mage Invisiblique.* For this I need the assistance of two gentlemen from the audience, if they will kindly grant me their help."

Monsieur Blitzini's eyes, which had been wandering fitfully during the delivery of this speech, now fell on Wyoming and Cameron, who waited for no further invitation, but sprang up the run-down and stood on the stage by his side.

"Thank you," continued Monsieur Blitzini, bowing. Wyoming thought he detected a fleeting expression of relief on the conjurer's face, as though he was glad to have some one near him to come to his aid in case of need.

"The beginning of this experiment is very simple; it is only the end which is strangely startling and inexpressibly surprising. I put a pack of cards on the centre-table here. Then I stand on this little table with the glass top and I ask these gentlemen to cover me over with this extinguisher, in order that I may be wholly unable to see what may take place on the stage. Then one gentleman will count thirty seconds, while the other gentleman takes a card from the pack, looks at it, shows it to you, and returns it. At the end of the half-minute both gentlemen lift the tall cone and release me from my solitary confinement in this dark cell. Then I will declare the card which the gentleman drew. First I ask the two gentlemen to examine this little table."

The two friends looked at it carefully. It was very simple in construction; it had three light steel legs, and it had a top of thick plate-glass. They declared themselves quite satisfied.

Monsieur Blitzini turned to the extinguisher, and as he stood beside it he was at least eighteen inches less in height than it was.

" Please examine this also," he said, tapping it with his finger. " You will see that it is very light, that it is made of several thicknesses of tough paper, and that there are no holes in it through which I can see."

Wyoming lifted the cone up and held it against the light, and he saw no holes in it. Then he and Cameron scrutinized the external surface thoroughly. At last they declared themselves satisfied again.

"Very well," said Monsieur Blitzini; "then we will proceed at once. You understand what is to be done? I am to be covered for exactly thirty seconds, during which time one of you is to take a card from the pack, show it to the audience, and return it, leaving the pack in exactly its original position."

The two friends told him that they understood what was required of them.

"Then here goes," said Monsieur Blitzini, and although he was obviously trying to keep his voice steady, there was a distinct tremor in it. Placing both hands on the little table, he sprang upon it and stood erect. Wyoming and Cameron mounted on chairs, one on his right and one on his left; they raised the huge cone from the floor and slowly lowered it over him. It rested lightly on the rim of the little table.

Wyoming drew out his watch and began counting the seconds. Cameron stepped down from his chair, crossed to the large table in the centre of the stage, selected a card from the pack, glanced at it, showed it, returned it, and replaced the pack as it was. Then he walked back and mounted his chair again. Wyoming had stood motionless, with his eyes on the dial and his ears strained to catch the slightest sound.

At last he returned his watch to his pocket, saying, " Time's up! "

Then he and Cameron, amid a dead silence in the hall, seized the extinguisher and lifted it slowly. As it rose in the air, they heard a sudden murmur of astonishment among the audience. In another second, as they lowered the light paper cone to the stage, they saw the cause of this. The little table whereon Monsieur Blitzini had stood was empty. The magician had vanished; he had gone without a sign or a sound; it was as though he had melted into air.

Wyoming and Cameron examined the extinguisher, but it was no heavier than it had been, nor was the little table in any way altered. The spectators clapped and shouted with delight at this most original trick. The two friends looked at each other in surprise. After exchanging puzzled glances, they stepped down from the chairs on which they had been standing, and again examined the little table and the cone. But they found no clue to the disappearance of the magician.

Then there arose from the body of the hall a loud cry for the conjurer to appear. It was a hearty and genuine call such as few of the strolling actors who have starred at the Pavilion had ever been honored with.

"Fetch him out," said Wyoming to Cameron; "you know the topography of the place."

Cameron crossed at once to the two dressing-rooms on the right of the stage, whence Monsieur Blitzini had issued at the beginning of the performance. Wyoming heard him knocking, and then opening a door. He said a few words to the impatient spectators, suggesting that they should give

Monsieur Blitzini breathing-time after his extraordinary exertions.

The audience took this in good part. There was a cessation of the loud shouts and tumultuous applause. Then in a minute Cameron came back, looking flushed and scared.

"He's not there," he whispered to Wyoming.

"Then where is he?" asked the American, startled and with a sinking heart.

"I don't know. I've searched the stage and the two dressing-rooms and the short passages, and I'm sure he is not here."

"How could he get out? You told me there was no stage-door."

"And there is no space under the stage where he could hide. I do not understand it at all. Perhaps your spooks——"

But here Cameron was interrupted by impatient cries from the audience, who wanted to see the conjurer.

Wyoming stepped forward to the centre of the stage, and made a neat little speech to the spectators, in the course of which he said that Monsieur Blitzini had evidently determined that his last trick should be a complete success and a total surprise, and that to this end he had chosen to vanish. He concluded by expressing his belief that they all appreciated the remarkable skill and address that Monsieur Blitzini had revealed that evening.

The audience gave Wyoming a round of applause, and broke up in high good-humor.

The two friends returned to their hotel, musing much and saying little.

"Do you understand the deep damnation of his taking off?" asked Wyoming, as they parted for the night.

"Not the least bit. Do you?"

"No."

At breakfast the next morning Cameron passed the Witherington *Daily Times* across the table to Wyoming, and asked him to read the final paragraph of the local reporter's account of the strange events of the preceding evening.

"Whether Mons. Blitzini," so this paragraph began, "derives his extraordinary command over *légerdemain,* as our lively neighbors call it, from the abnormal sources set forth in his advertisement, or no, is a philosophical conundrum upon which we need not enter now. *Credat Judæus Apelles.* But besides his being a juggler of no mean proficiency, he is undoubtedly a humorist of the first water. Trick after trick was transmogrified in the most whimsical and facetious fashion, and the admirable facial powers which Mons. Blitzini exhibited in depicting emotions of surprise and consternation, contributed not a little to this effect. He well deserved the applause lavished on him continuously, and the excitement of the intelligent and brilliant audience knew no bounds when the extinguisher, which played an important part in the last trick, was removed, and Mons. Blitzini was found to have vanished in the twinkling of an eye. We can confidently recommend all who like an exhibition of finished skill and a hearty laugh to attend Mons. Blitzini's second performance, advertised in our columns for to-night. We hope, however, that on this occasion he will not carry his invisibility so far as to refuse appearing to receive the plaudits of the admiring audience he has so cleverly amused."

Wyoming read this carefully, then he laid the paper on the table and said: "This reporter seems to be a good many kinds of a fool."

"I suppose we shall go to-night to see Monsieur Blitzini's second performance?" asked Cameron.

"Of course," was the American's short reply.

CHAPTER II.

MONSIEUR BLITZINI'S SECOND PERFORMANCE.

MONSIEUR BLITZINI'S second performance never took place.

MATED BY MAGIC.

(In Collaboration with Walter Herries Pollock.)

11

MATED BY MAGIC.

A STORY WITH A POSTSCRIPT.

I.

THE STORY.

WHEN Steele Wyoming arrived at his customary apartments in Half Moon Street, Piccadilly, one morning early in June, he found a telegram awaiting him from Cecil Cameron. As was his wont, Wyoming, having left New York about the 1st of May on a steamer of the French line, had been spending a month in Paris, rambling through the Salon, going to all the many smaller exhibitions, seeing all the shows of all sorts, from the Théâtre Français to Neuilly Fair, and giving himself up to the lazy enjoyment a cultivated American can always attain in the city by the Seine. But when the race for the Grand Prix had been run, and when the theatres began to close their doors, he wrote over to London asking that his rooms be made ready; and about the time when the Queen's birthday is celebrated, Wyoming took the night train and arrived in London before the city by the Thames was yet awake.

Early as it was, the telegram from Cecil Cameron had arrived before him. While his trunks were being taken into his room, he tore open the brown envelope and read this message:

"Steele Wyoming, 51 Half Moon Street, Piccadilly.

"Welcome, Rosicrucian Brother! I want you to call spooks from the vasty deep. Lunch at Babel Club at one. You hear my horn?　　CECIL CAMERON."

Wyoming held the telegram in his hand for a moment.

"That man makes me tired," he said to himself, "with his mania for trying to talk American. Why can't he be content with his own insular and parochial dialect? But he's a good fellow, for all that."

The American's face was even more solemn than usual as he laid the dispatch on the table.

"I wonder what mischief he is up to now," was his reflection. "Raising spooks is always fun, however, and he can count me in."

So it was that Wyoming went to the Babel Club to meet his friend at the appointed hour. The Babel Club, as all must know, was founded as a place of meeting for men who could speak at least three modern languages. Cecil Cameron, proud of his proficiency, offered the American language as one of his three. As he spoke French and German

in addition to English, he was admitted. To prevent a confusion of tongues, there was an unwritten
law of the club by which a member making use of
any foreign word was fined elevenpence halfpenny.

As Steele Wyoming was about to take his seat
at the little table in the bow window which juts out
into Piccadilly, Cecil Cameron entered the dining-
room.

"How are you, old man?" asked the American.

"I am able to sit up and take nourishment," replied the Englishman. "And how are you?"

"I'm not the better for the privilege of listening
to your vain efforts to mimic our noble American
language," was Wyoming's prompt reply. "Why
are you not content with the dialect spoken by the
inhabitants of Great Britain and her colonial de-
pendencies?"

"Because I prefer the pictorial freedom of speech
which echoes over the boundless prairies of the
mighty West," Cameron returned.

"Well," said Wyoming, with a weary sigh, "push
forward to your own destruction. Linguistic pit-
falls are on all sides of you. No man can speak
American who is not born in the purple of American sovereignty. So I forgive you; and I may as
well confess that I'd liever hear an energetic Amer-

icanism, now and again, than the enervating Briticisms which besprinkle the speech of most of you
fellows over here.   Now drive on your donkey-cart
and tell me about the spirits."

" Do you know my Australian cousin, Frank
Hardy ? " asked Cameron.

" No," the American replied.   " Do you want to
scare up a spook or two for him ? "

" Frank Hardy is in love with the only daughter
of J. Bulstrode-Travis, Esq., of Redrose Hall,
Flintshire."

" Then he doesn't need anybody to raise his
spirits, I take it," ventured the American.

" Frank's all right," Cameron returned; " he's all
wool and a yard wide ! "

" Has the girl gone back on him ? " asked Wyoming.

" No," said the Englishman.   " Lavinia is as much
in love with Frank as Frank is with her."

" Well, then ? "

" There is the cruel parient.   He is worth £30,-
000 a year and Frank hasn't a red cent."

" Then he'd better pass in his checks, hadn't he ? "
Wyoming inquired, dropping into American slang,
as he did inevitably when he talked to Cameron.

" Here is where we can help.   The young people

have not dared to tell the old man the state of their feelings. He suspects nothing. He is very ambitious for his daughter. He would like her to be at least a countess. But he is also a little daft on the subject of spiritualism, and he has been going in for fads like——"

"One moment, if you please, Cecil," interrupted Wyoming. "As I warned you, the linguistic man-trap has you by the heel. 'To go in for' and 'fad' are Briticisms of the most British kind."

"I know it," Cameron admitted sorrowfully. "But yours is such a difficult tongue to acquire. Where was I?"

"You were saying that the girl's father was a man of many left-handed ideas."

"That's it exactly. On some subjects he is like the rest of us, and on others he is very eccentric," the Englishman continued.

"And in mechanics," said the American, "the eccentric is often very near a crank."

"In some ways he is cranky indeed," Cameron replied. "He is an enthusiastic chess-player for one thing—though he doesn't play remarkably."

"But what have I to do with this estimable country gentleman?" asked the American.

"Only this. Mr. Bulstrode-Travis is a fatalist,

a believer in signs and wonders, a practitioner of thought-reading, an interpreter of dreams, and so forth. Now, Frank knew that I was a student of modern magic and that I took no stock in spookical research. So he came to me and confided his plight, and asked me to help him out. Frank thinks that I can show the old man some strange marvel, and then ring in on him a prediction of some sort pointing to Frank as the only proper husband for Lavinia."

" Work the oracle, in short ? "

" Precisely. And I have said I would; and I want you to help me as a member of the Rosicrucian Brotherhood. Mr. Bulstrode-Travis has been up in town for a week, and although he has two old-fogy clubs of his own, the Mausoleum and the Sarcophagus, I got him put down here as a guest, and I coaxed him to come here, and I prevailed on two or three good-natured fellows to play chess with him and get beaten, so the old boy drops in here pretty freely. He and I are excellent friends. We talk over the mysteries of magic and thought-trans-ference, and I am properly serious. He has asked me to run down with him to Redrose Hall to spend Saturday and Sunday. I have spoken to him about you, representing that you had been a profound student of strange rites; I said that I had been told that you had investigated the Eleusinian mysteries; I knew you had been present at a Voodoo exorcising; and I had seen you extract extraordinary information as to the future by means of the *sortes Virgiliana*. In fact, he takes you for a boss spook-stalker."

"Well?" asked the American, with an expression of solemnity, not to say gloom.

"If he comes here to lunch to-day, we drop into a chat together; and if he doesn't ask you down to the Hall to spend Saturday and Sunday, then I haven't any savvy."

"Well?" repeated Wyoming.

"And once down there we'll raise the devil for him, or the Witch of Endor, or the Witches of Macbeth; and we'll make them prophesy the union of Lavinia and Frank."

"I see," said the American; "and it's a very pretty scheme if it works—but——"

"Hush!" Cameron interrupted. "Here he is!"

The broad door of the dining-room had opened to give passage to a handsome, portly old gentleman, bearing his sixty years bravely. This was Mr. Bulstrode-Travis. Cameron introduced Wyoming, successfully suggesting by his manner that he was presenting a man of marvel.

Mr. Bulstrode-Travis sat down to lunch with them, and before long the three were in full cry over mystery and magic. Wyoming and Cameron played into each other's hands so as to hint dimly to the old gentleman that they were in some strange and secret way familiar with the personalities of Cornelius Agrippa, Paracelsus, Faust, Robert Houdin, the Egyptian magicians, Count Cagliostro, Arbaces, and various other engaging persons. Cameron related a tale which, as it happened, he had actually heard from an imaginative doctor, who said he had lived as a medical student in Bulwer-Lytton's haunted house in Orchard Street, and that among other things they never wanted ("needed" interjected Wyoming with soft correction) any artificial light at night-fall, as an Unseen Power kindly provided it. Wyoming capped the story with an American tale of his own, the incidents of which he said had actually befallen him. Then they alluded casually, but frequently, to the wonders they had sometimes worked in conjunction. Mr. Bulstrode-Travis was in an ecstasy at the idea of such strange doings; he burned to see what they had seen and what they could accomplish; and therefore it was with peculiar cordiality that he asked Wyoming to accompany Cameron on his visit to Redrose Hall.

The invitation was accepted with unaffected prompt-
ness, and Wyoming, thinking, unwisely perhaps, to
add a touch, said mournfully:

"We could have shown you more had poor Monsieur Blitzini been here."

"But you know, Steele," replied Cameron, in a
frivolous moment, "it's no good wishing—he's gone
up the flume !"

"Ah," rejoined Wyoming dryly, "he really speaks
American like a native—sometimes."

Redrose Hall stands on high ground, encircled or
supported by lawns and a pretty succession of fish-
ponds. Part of the house is really Elizabethan, the
other part is skilfully arranged to match it. A car-
riage-drive sweeps up to a fine porch, through which
one passes into a hall hung with armor, thence into
an anteroom, at the left corner and end of which
are respectively the dining-room and the drawing-
room. In front of the drawing-room runs a terrace
with a plashing fountain. At the further end of the
drawing-room is a conservatory leading to the hang-
ing-gardens, and at right angles to this the double
door of the library. Coming out of the library into
the anteroom one sees opposite the drawing-room
a wide staircase leading to a gallery of bedrooms.

Mr. Bulstrode-Travis, whose fussy and interjectional manner belied his appearance, which was that of the fine old English gentleman, conducted our two friends to the drawing-room, with much pleasing prattle about his small but excellent collection of armor and weapons, and about his library of magical and cabalistic books which, handsomely arranged in glass cases, adorned the walls of the anteroom.

" Here is a pretty edition of Gabriel Hervey, eh ? " he would say, or " Do but look, Mr. Wyoming, at this Reginald Scot, ha ? "

The two friends lingered awhile in the library, where Frank Hardy soon joined them. Mr. Bulstrode-Travis and Wyoming chatted about books, leaving Hardy and Cameron to a game of piquet.

In the drawing-room, whither the host soon conducted the American, they found Miss Bulstrode-Travis, to whom Wyoming took a great fancy. Among the other guests were Sir Kensington Gower, K.C.B., and Lady Gower, Lord Luine a great traveller who had been much in India and took stock, as Cameron would have said, in fakirs and such like and Mrs. Vendale, a slight, short, fantastic creature who believed, or affected to believe, in Khoot-Hoomi.

In the drawing-room the conversation was of rain and fine time, but at dinner it soon took on it a color of magical lore. Wyoming was seated next to Lavinia, and they got on capitally. The English girl thought the American amusing, and the American found the English girl bright and sympathetic. After dinner the party moved to the conservatory, where coffee was served and where smoking was always permitted.

Mrs. Vendale asked Lord Luine if the wonders of the Indian magicians were authentic—" For my part, I do not doubt it ; but perhaps they use *black* magic, and that would be horrible."

Luine replied that he cared much more about tracking a tiger than about seeing a trick or a portent. " But, don't you know, I have seen those fellows do things that no person " (he was a Scotchman) " could explain."

Then he recounted the mango trick and the basket trick, and added that the Indian conjurers had nothing on practically but a waist-cloth, and how could they hide things ?

Cameron and Wyoming looked at each other.

Then Luine related how he had seen a man climb up a rope until you lost sight of him, and he never came down again. Luine was a man of absolute veracity, but at this the two did *not* look at each other.

There was much serious conversation on this, broken only by a frivolous remark of Cameron's to Wyoming.

"Say, Steele, that Louis XV. clock reminds me of your watch that I had to wrap in a blanket at night when we travelled together because it ticked so loud.   Have you got it yet?"

"Yes, I have it," said Wyoming, "but don't let your mind wander."

Mr. Bulstrode-Travis's appetite for the wonderful began to grow by what it fed on, and he made such broken requests as "Couldn't you, hey?—wouldn't it be possible—what?—when two people of such remarkable powers, and, as is evident, so completely *en rapport* with each other—it seems a pity, you know."

The two friends made excuses and demurs until the old gentleman was near to dancing with unsatisfied expectation, and then when the rest of the party joined themselves to Mr. Bulstrode-Travis in polite importunity, they consented, with a show of giving way gracefully, to see if the conditions would enable them to accomplish anything.

"Of course, you have heard," said Wyoming, "about what is called thought-reading?"

"A very primitive form," added Cameron, and went on to say, "Steele, will you try if our old experiment together can be worked? That is to say, I will leave the room, and shall try to gather from your magnetism, without word or touch, what action the company may wish me to perform."

Mr. Bulstrode-Travis's eyes opened wide at this, and the suggestion was received with such delight that Mrs. Vendale's "they do say that the Chelahs——" perished unachieved.

When Cameron left the room there was a complete silence for a moment.

"Seems to me," said Luine, "we'd better decide upon what we want the noble sportsman to do. Finding a pin is played out. Set him something more difficult."

"Suppose," said Mrs. Vendale, with the tone of a languishing spectre, "suppose we were to move that beautiful vase up to the blue room, and will him to find it and bring it down again?"

"Might break it if he found it," said Sir Kensington.

"Do you think, Sir Kensington—hey?" answered the host, "that I value a vase one penny in comparison with the interest of science?"

"Don't spoil the fun, my dear," added Lady Gower, a pleasing and vivacious person.

"Is that, then, what you all wish?" said Wyoming, and was answered by universal assent.

"Now," Wyoming went on, "let me carry the vase to the blue room and hide it somewhere in concert with Lord Luine, who will watch that there may be no possible collusion between my friend and myself."

Lord Luine rose to accompany him.

'Add one thing more," said Wyoming. "Cameron ought to be blindfolded, the lights must be put out, and only one of our party must carry a dark lantern to prevent our stumbling. *He* won't stumble if it succeeds."

Upon this Wyoming took the vase in his hands and left the conservatory, accompanied by Lord Luine. They went to the blue room, and after much deliberation Wyoming placed the vase on a bracket so high on the wall that a tall man could barely reach it.

As they went out Luine stopped at the door and said, "But look here, he *will* break the vase if it's so high up as that."

"No, sir," said Wyoming, "but to make assurance doubly sure I'll measure it once again." He took three steps back to the bracket, picked up a small pin-cushion from a table close by, and with some difficulty placed it on the bracket.

"Cameron is not so tall as you are," said Luine.

"No matter," Wyoming rejoined, "he will not break it."

Then they went back to the conservatory, and Cameron was called in. Amid intense silence Wyoming looked him full in the eyes for about two minutes, when there stole over Cameron a dazed yet awakened look of a curious kind.

"Hush!" cried Wyoming, "the charm works. Now let him go; we will follow after at some ten yards' distance."

"But if he falls and hurts himself?" said Sir Kensington.

"Hush!" said Wyoming, authoritatively. "He will not fall. Now!"

Cameron, who had been standing motionless, suddenly strode to the door, opened it, went straight through the drawing-room, opened that door, and walked into the now darkened anteroom. Here he paused awhile. Frank Hardy, holding the dark lantern, with silent gestures kept back the eager followers.

At last Cameron opened the library door, walked

12

round, and came straight out again, and made immediately for the staircase, mounted it, and passed into the gallery until he reached the blue room, of which he at once opened the door. Then were there murmurs from those who watched him like those to be heard when fireworks are let off. As soon as he had opened this door Cameron shut it again, and stood outside it in hesitation. Then he went down the gallery and tried every door with intense deliberation. When he had done this he stood again as one in doubt, and then again ran as hard as he could to the blue room, opened the door, and rushed in. Hardy followed with the lantern, holding it so that those behind could see what happened. What happened was this: Cameron went to the bracket, put his left hand against the wall, straightened himself up as if by a great effort, and just reached the base of the vase with his right hand.

" He'll break it," whispered Sir Kensington, upon whom his wife turned a look of scorn, which missed its effect because he did not see it.

Very carefully and slowly Cameron took down the vase without the slightest appearance of risk; but when he had it safe, as it seemed, in both his hands, he shivered and tottered so that Wyoming, who was nearest to him, rushed forward to save the vase, and supporting it with one hand laid the other heavily on Cameron's shoulder, as if to infuse new magnetism into him.

From that moment Cameron's descent to the conservatory was a triumphal march. There was no longer any question of managing the dark lan- tern, and people hesitated not to wonder in loud voices if he would restore the vase to its original place—which he did at once and without hesitation.

Having completed his appointed task, Cameron sank exhausted in an arm-chair, gazing into vacancy, and then quite suddenly gave a shiver, sat up, looked round him, and fixed his eyes interroga- tively on Wyoming, who answered with a quiet nod. Then the silence which had fallen on the company when Cameron sat down was broken, and the chorus of comments, questions, answers, expressions of admiration, were even as the "confused noise without" of the drama. This lasted some time, until the company, like tigers having tasted blood (or, to make the simile more exact, like the people without consciences who encore singers), began to suggest "if it were possible," "Mr. Cameron must be tired, and yet if," and so forth, and so forth. One young lady, who seemed not fully to understand the novelty of what she had just seen, wanted to know if Mr. Cameron could do a card trick next — she doted on tricks with cards.

"That gives me an idea," said Wyoming. "Cards suggest chess, you know. Have you a chess-board in the house?"

"Chess-boards—hey?" said Mr. Bulstrode-Travis, "heaps of 'em—what?—how many do you want?"

"One will be enough," replied Wyoming.

"What is it for?" asked little Mrs. Vendale, in tones which were both hard and caressing.

Wyoming refrained from saying "to play chess with," and answered instead, "You will see directly. Does any one present besides our host play chess?"

Luine and Sir Kensington answered that they played a little.

"That is enough," said Wyoming.

"What are you up to now?" Cameron inquired.

"What are you going to do?" asked Mr. Bulstrode-Travis, with the double delight in the anticipated commingling of chess and mystery.

"I don't know that we can do anything," replied the American. "In fact, so far as I know, nothing of this sort has ever been attempted before. Thought-reading, even in its highest phases, requires proximity, and the test I propose now will be at a distance quite unprecedented."

"You might at least tell me what you are driving at," said Cameron.

Wyoming faced him suddenly. "Do you think we could communicate to each other the moves of a game of chess by will-power alone?" he said.

"I see," Cameron answered. Then, after a pause, he added, "We might try it."

"This is what I propose, then," cried Wyoming, "to have the board on this table here, watched by two of the party, while a third makes the moves."

"What moves?" asked Mrs. Vendale again.

"The moves which will be conveyed by message from Cameron and myself, who will be each respectively shut up in a dark room, the two rooms to be as far from each other as possible."

The audacity of the proposal so startled the assemblage that scarcely anything was said until the arrangements were complete. A chess-board was placed on the table in the centre of the conservatory, and, aided by Lavinia, Mr. Bulstrode-Travis nervously arranged the pieces. Then he took an arm-chair alongside the table and sat down to watch the game.

" I'll give you the choice of colors, as I suggested the game," said Wyoming.

" I try to act like a white man, as you Americans say," Cameron replied, "and so I'll take them."

"Very well," Wyoming returned.   " I'm quite satisfied with the black men; the colored troops can fight nobly, if need be."

Then Cameron and Wyoming were stationed in darkened rooms ten yards or more apart, while one of the company remained with each of them, a third standing sentry in the corridor between.

Luine, who was with Cameron, came back to the conservatory and made the first move for White— Pawn to Queen's Bishop's fourth.

At this unconventional beginning Mr. Bulstrode-Travis smiled and said, " Evidently we are to have a surprise opening."

As Luine left the room to rejoin Cameron, Sir Kensington, who was Wyoming's messenger, entered the conservatory, and walking to the table made Black's first move, Knight to Queen's Bishop's third.

" A strange attack calls for strange precautions," was the host's comment on this.

Having made the move, Sir Kensington returned to Wyoming.

A few seconds after he had left the conservatory Luine reappeared and made White's second move, Queen to Bishop's second.

"The Queen looks out at the window," said Lavinia, smiling; she was almost as interested in the game as her father.

After Luine had disappeared, Sir Kensington returned, bearing Black's retort, Pawn to Queen's fourth.

"Is this defence or defiance?" queried Frank Hardy, leaning over Lavinia's chair.

Then Luine came with Cameron's third move, Knight to Queen's Bishop's third.

"Good!" cried Mr. Bulstrode-Travis. "We shall see all his meaning soon." And he watched eagerly the departure of Cameron's emissary and the arrival of Wyoming's, who moved a Black Knight to Queen's fifth.

"Well, he takes the bull by the horns," was the instant remark of the chess enthusiast.

And so the moves followed, without any communication between the players, who remained each in his dark room, never speaking, except to whisper to his companion the move he desired to have made on the table in the conservatory.

"This is more than a blindfold game," said Mr.

Bulstrode-Travis, as White's fourth move, Queen to Rook's fourth, was made, giving check. "It is a double blindfold game, complicated by the strange and altogether mysterious sympathy or intuition or occult influence which transmits to each the move the other has made. Easily parried," he cried, as Black sent forward a Pawn to Queen's Bishop's third.

"He must have a deep motive, but I don't see it," was Mr. Bulstrode-Travis's remark when Luine made White's fifth move, Knight to Queen's square. And when Sir Kensington promptly appeared and sent forward a Pawn to Queen's Knight's fourth, Lavinia looked at her father in surprise, and he answered her silent query, "It's either courage or impudence, and I'm sure I don't know which. I'm astonished at the whole affair. I think the game is almost as wonderful as the way they are playing it."

The sixth move was watched with an increasing interest. Luine appeared, and the White Pawn took the Black Pawn, and Luine disappeared. Then Sir Kensington appeared, the Black Pawn went to Queen's Bishop's fourth, and Sir Kensington disappeared.

"Evidently he despises the attack," commented Mr. Bulstrode-Travis, who was leaning forward in his chair, with both his elbows on the table which held the chess-board.

There seemed to be even a shorter interval than usual after Sir Kensington left the conservatory before Luine entered it, to make White's seventh move, Pawn to Knight's sixth, discovering check. And as swiftly came Sir Kensington back with Wyoming's adroit retort, Bishop to Queen's second.

"Where is White's Queen to go?" asked Mr. Bulstrode-Travis. "What can White do now— what?"

And White could do no more in effect. In the next move the White Queen was taken, and then Luine came in to say that Mr. Cameron resigned the game. Lavinia went to bear the news of his victory to Wyoming, and to call him in to receive their congratulations.

"It is the most wonderful feat I ever saw!" cried Mr. Bulstrode-Travis, springing up from his seat with excitement, as Cameron came back, summoned by Luine. "I have never even heard of anything like it! Are you exhausted by the nervous strain?"

"It is wearing on the gray matter of the brain," Cameron replied, "but I shall get my breath in a minute or two."

" And you, Mr. Wyoming," said the host to the American, who returned with Lavinia. " You have played an absolutely unprecedented game in an absolutely unprecedented way. I confess that I don't see how you do it--what !"

" Really, I don't know that I could explain it exactly to your satisfaction," Wyoming answered. " I suppose I can say that it is a reading of each other's mind."

" It must be a great convenience to be able to read other people's minds," said Lavinia. " I think I should like it."

" I'm sure that you would never find anything but pleasant thoughts toward you," Wyoming returned.

Her father was already moving across the conservatory to Cameron. " Thought-reading applied to chess and performed under test conditions which preclude the possibility of deception—that's what I call it," he said with oratorical emphasis.

" Well," Cameron replied quietly, " you may call it that."

" Is your friend a married man ?" asked Mr. Bulstrode-Travis, suddenly dropping his voice into a mysterious whisper.

"Wyoming! indeed, no; he's a bachelor of the deepest dye," Cameron replied.

"And in your reading of his thoughts have you yet discovered that his affections are engaged?" pursued the host.

"Why? What do you mean?" Cameron asked.

"Look there!" said Lavinia's father, with a gesture indicating Wyoming leaning over the young lady in pleasant conversation. "I do not know that I should object."

"Object to what?" cried Cameron in sudden alarm.

"Object to your friend for a son-in-law," said Mr. Bulstrode-Travis. "He seems to be taken with Lavinia."

"I hope not!" ejaculated Cameron. Then, recovering himself, he added: "I had a suspicion that Frank Hardy was rather attentive to her."

"No doubt, no doubt," said Lavinia's father; "but I do not think she thinks of him—and that is what's important, you know."

"You surprise me," Cameron continued. "I had supposed that she had rather a liking for him."

"Did you read that in her mind?" asked her father eagerly. "That would be very curious indeed—what!"

"Yes," Cameron rejoined gravely; "it would be very curious indeed." Then he saw his chance. "If you would like to inquire into the future—to consult an oracle, in fact—you might get Wyoming to do the *sortes Virgilianæ* for you."

"To be sure," cried Mr. Bulstrode-Travis. "You told me he was an expert. Do you know, I never saw the attempt made."

"My friend has a method of his own, quite different from that which is down in the books," Cameron explained. "I say, Steele," he cried, "Mr. Bulstrode-Travis would like to see you cast the *sortes.*"

Wyoming crossed the room and joined them. "And what is the question to which you seek an answer?" he asked.

Mr. Bulstrode-Travis hesitated; but Cameron, lowering his voice, responded for him: "The others need not know exactly the object of our question, but our host would like guidance in regard to his daughter's future husband."

"I see," the American rejoined. "Why not?"

"Why not, indeed?" echoed Lavinia's father. "If you will kindly lend me your skill—what!"

"I will do what I can," Wyoming replied. "Have you a Virgil?"

"Lavinia, my dear, will you bring me the Virgil from the library? It is in that long set of classic texts to the left of the fireplace."

"I know where it is, Papa," said his daughter as she arose and left the room.

"And then I shall need a pack of cards," Wyoming went on.

"A pack of cards—what?" echoed Mr. Bulstrode Travis.

"There's a pack in the library," Cameron cried. "Hardy and I were playing piquet before dinner. I'll get them."

When Lavinia returned with the Virgil, Wyoming begged her to keep it for the moment. He requested everybody to sit down. It was with difficulty that he was able to keep Mr. Bulstrode-Travis quiet. In the end, however, the company had taken seats, Frank Hardy seizing the occasion to claim the place next to Lavinia. They were grouped in an irregular crescent, with Lavinia in the centre and her father on one of the horns.

At last Cameron came back with the cards. "I've looked over them, old man," he said, "and I've no doubt that you will find them all right."

Wyoming took the pack, and, running through it

hastily, he selected twelve hearts, the Ace to the Ten, with the Knave and Queen.

"I have here," he explained, "twelve numbers, counting the Knave as eleven and the Queen as twelve. And there are twelve books of the ' Æneid.' I will shuffle these dozen cards, and take them to Mrs. Vendale and ask her to draw one."

"Must I choose without seeing what it is?" Mrs. Vendale asked.

"Take any one," answered Wyoming, fanning them out before her.

"Then I select this one," she said, picking out the card which the American had kept persistently before her.

"What is it?" cried Mr. Bulstrode-Travis.

"It is the Seven of Hearts," she answered.

"The seven—a sacred number—a most fortunate choice," said Wyoming. "Now, Miss Lavinia, will you kindly turn to the seventh book of the ' Æneid,' which has thus been dictated to us?"

"I see—I see," commented the host. "You have found the book from which the mystic line is to be taken; but how do you find the line itself?"

"You shall see in a moment," responded the American. "I shall distribute five of these cards to different persons present—to Sir Kensington and to Lady Gower, to Mrs. Vendale, to Hardy, and to you, Cecil. And I ask you to write down a number, any whole number you please between one and a hundred, without any consultation with each other."

In a minute more the five numbers were written. Wyoming went from one to the other collecting the cards, which he placed on the top of the pack. Then he went down the line to Mr. Bulstrode-Travis and handed him five cards. To Frank Hardy, who was watching Wyoming's every move, it seemed as though these cards came from the bottom of the pack; but this was apparently a mistake, as the host took the five cards, saying, " And what am I to do with these numbers ? "

"You are to add them together in absolute silence," replied Wyoming; "and I must request that no one speaks until the result is announced. It is essential that there should now be nothing to distract the attention."

For a moment there was no sound to be heard save the scraping of a pencil in the hand of the host, as he copied the numbers out on one card and added them up.

" I make it two hundred and fifty-five," he said at last.

"Then," and Wyoming spoke with his most impressive manner, "I have to request Miss Lavinia to turn to the two hundred and fifty-fifth line of the seventh book of the 'Æneid.'"

"I see now," cried Mr. Bulstrode-Travis; "a most ingenious method, and absolutely free from any possible personal influence, as we all collaborated in bringing it about, although of course in different degrees."

"I have the line," said Lavinia.

"Then if Mr. Hardy will kindly read it to us," Wyoming went on.

"Certainly, if you wish it," Hardy replied, but when his eye fell on the line he flushed and hesitated. Then mastering his surprise he read:

Hunc illum fatis externa ab sede profectum
Portendi generum.

"And what does that gibberish mean?" asked Mrs. Vendale abruptly.

"It means that the old King of Latium had come to the conclusion that the stranger who had arrived from across the sea was the son-in-law foretold by the fates," Cameron explained.

And Wyoming, leaning over the back of Mr. Bulstrode-Travis's chair, whispered, "*Hunc gene-*

rum—this is the son-in-law," and he indicated Frank Hardy. "He comes over sea, as he is an Australian; and, as you may remember, the name of the king's daughter was Lavinia."

"So it was," said Mr. Bulstrode-Travis, who recalled his Virgil but vaguely. "Really this is a most extraordinary coincidence, or manifestation, or what shall I call it?"

"Do not disregard so solemn a message from the fates," the American rejoined gravely. "If your daughter will have this young Australian, the sooner you make the match the better."

And so it came about, and in due season the *Morning Post* announced that a marriage had been arranged between Lavinia, the only daughter of Mr. Bulstrode-Travis, of Redrose Hall, Flintshire, and Mr. Frank Hardy, who had recently returned from Australia. As there was no reason for delay the wedding was set for early in August.

13

II.

THE POSTSCRIPT.

It so happened that Cameron and Wyoming were in town when the wedding took place, and that they were invited to go to the railway station from which the young people were about to start on their wedding tour.   Both Frank and Lavinia felt that their happiness was due in great measure to the effort of the two friends, and they were prompt in expressing their gratitude.   The young couple were in their carriage, while Cameron and Wyoming leaned in at the window.   Already the guard's voice was heard, and the departure of the train was imminent.

"Tell me one thing," cried the bridegroom, at last summoning courage.   "How did you do the chess game ?   That has puzzled me ever since."

Cameron and Wyoming laughed.

"Is that the only one of our feats which puzzles you ?" asked the American.

"Yes," replied Hardy, "I think it is.   At least I can guess at the others.   I know that he found the vase in the blue room by the ticking of your watch, and I think that I saw you give my respected father-in-law not the cards we had written numbers on, but others with the numbers Cecil had prepared in advance."

"Oh, oh!" said Cameron; "it seems we have a promising neophyte here for the Rosicrucian Brotherhood."

"But the chess game?" Hardy continued; "there I am puzzled. I don't see it at all. How did you do it?"

Here the guard warned the two friends away from the door of the compartment, and already the first tremor of motion was felt in the train.

"This is our last request!" cried Lavinia. "How did you do it?"

Wyòming looked at Cameron, who nodded. Then he said, quietly, "We made up the game in advance, and learnt it by heart."

"Oh!" said Hardy.

And the train started sharply forward, and bore the young couple swiftly out of sight to the happiness of a honeymoon.

ONE STORY IS GOOD TILL ANOTHER IS TOLD,

(In Collaboration with Geo. H. Jessop.)

ONE STORY IS GOOD TILL ANOTHER IS TOLD.

I.

THE STATEMENT OF MR. LEROY HOWARD.

Prepared by Himself.

I MUST premise that I know of no reason whatever for the violent assault committed upon me last evening by the brutal Irish ruffian now under arrest. Nor can I imagine any excuse of any kind, save the promptings of his evil nature and the natural turbulence of his race. The attack was absolutely unexpected, and it was wholly unprovoked. So far as I am aware, I had never even laid eyes on the hulking brute five minutes before he rushed across the street and assaulted me. I know nothing whatever of this Tim Dwyer save that I have been the victim of a cruel and cowardly outrage at his hands.

I do not exactly understand the report which is brought to me by my lawyer as to this Dwyer's assertions, and I am unable precisely to meet an allegation most vaguely worded. But there seems to be some sort of an assertion that the photograph I took by the flash light in the dusk last evening, just before the wanton assault was made upon me, was not the first I had taken of him, and that in some way or other I had taken his picture at other times perforce and against his will. I have no doubt that such a man fears to find his brutal features ex-posed in the Rogue's Gallery, but I have had neither part nor lot in any such task, useful to the com-munity as it may be.

To make this perfectly plain, and to destroy any credence which might otherwise be placed in the assertions of this foreign blackguard, I propose to set down here all the circumstances of my brief ex-periences as a photographer, from which it will be at once apparent there is not a shadow of a support for his allegation that I have in any way pursued or persecuted him. I shall prosecute him now, and I shall insist upon the infliction of the utmost pen-alty of the law. It will be a severe commentary on the lax administration of justice in this city if an inoffensive citizen is to be exposed to outrage at his very door, and if the brutal assailant can get off scot-free.

The facts of the case are as follows:

It is among the duties of my editorial position on the staff of *Youth*, a monthly magazine for boys and girls—a position I have held for now four months, since my graduation from the Oxbridge Grammar School—it is among my duties to assist in the art department of our publication. In the estimate of the young, pictures are of prime importance, and we pay especial attention to the proper illustration of the articles we publish. In the pursuance of this portion of my editorial duties I have familiarized myself with the most ingenious and interesting devices for securing photographs of animals in motion, and I have also given time to investigating the use of the " detective camera," commonly so called. As is known by all those whose obligations lead them to study the practical applications of the arts, this name is given to a simple and portable camera, so lightly made that it can be easily handled and unobtrusively carried; it is provided with machinery for taking an instantaneous photograph.

It was suggested to the editors of *Youth* that the charm of the unconscious movements of childhood might be caught and fixed by the so-called " detective camera," for the enjoyment and instruction of all who might see the pictures, and we were requested to consider the advisability of reproducing photographs of this character in the pages of *Youth* for the benefit of our readers. An editorial council was held to discuss this proposition, and it was declared feasible. One of the so-called "detective cameras" was ordered, and I was detailed to perfect myself in the art of taking instantaneous photographs.

On the day when the apparatus arrived at the house where I am boarding, No. 90 East Nineteenth Street, I happened to mention at the dinner-table the studies I was then engaged in, and the pleasant results we anticipated from the mission which had been confided to my charge. My friend Mr. Harry Brackett, one of the editors of the *Gotham Gazette*, who is a fellow-boarder of mine, immediately volunteered his assistance. I found that Mr. Brackett was familiar with the operation of the so-called "detective camera," and he volunteered to instruct me. The next morning, as it happened, was a Saturday, and there were several children in the house, who co-operated with us willingly. We went out into the rear yard, and as the young people frisked about innocently, Mr. Brackett and I succeeded in taking some half-dozen interesting and instructive groups and single figures. I may instance an instantaneous view of a game of hop-scotch, and another of three boys playing leap-frog, as distinct additions to our knowledge of the voluntary and involuntary movements of juvenile humanity. I was delighted with the results of our first day's labors, and I was anxious to proceed at once. But the next day was Sunday, and the day after was Monday, which happened to be the day when we close the forms of next month's number of *Youth*—and so I could not get to work again as speedily as I desired.

On Monday evening when Mr. Brackett took his seat beside me he told me that he had a new scheme, in which he wished my assistance. A friend had told him that a composition was now to be had the ignition of a small portion of which made a light so brilliant that it served for the taking of photographs. A little of this novel compound suddenly exploded by a percussion-cap made a flash, and the glare of this flash would suffice to imprint a picture on a sensitive plate adjusted properly on the so-called "detective camera." Mr. Brackett had procured a small can of this flashing powder, and he suggested that we go out that evening and take photographs in the dead of night. The idea had a distinct fascination, although I could not but doubt its prudence. I am not accustomed to wander at midnight through the highways and byways of a great city. But Mr. Brackett, having been formerly a reporter, whose privilege and duty it was to go everywhere and to know everybody, was eager for the proposed nocturnal excursion, and in time I suffered myself to be over-persuaded.

It was about ten o'clock on Monday night when we sallied forth in search of adventure. I confess that I was not without misgivings. The sky was cloudy, there was no moon, and it bade fair to rain. It was our intention to explore rather the less inhabited parts of the city, and especially the remains of what used to be known as Shanty Town. We took the Broadway cars to Central Park, and then we walked to Eighth Avenue and the Boulevard. As we turned the corner of an ill-paved street, in which there were but half a dozen houses on each side, we almost ran into a policeman. After a few words of explanation it was discovered that Mr. Brackett and the officer were old acquaintances. They had met when my friend had been detailed to work up police cases.

We were immediately warmly welcomed by the policeman, who was apparently of German birth, and seemingly a respectable person. He asked us what had brought us to so lonely a neighborhood at so strange an hour. Mr. Brackett then explained to him the object of our enterprise; he described to him the so-called "detective. camera," in which the officer expressed the greatest interest, evincing a strong desire to see its operation. He said that he was then about to arrest a minor malefactor, a man who had persisted in keeping poultry in violation of a city ordinance, and to the extreme annoyance of the neighbors. It seems that this man, after re-peated warnings, had suddenly hidden his hens from the sight of those who came to take him into cus-tody. That very morning, it appears, the officer had been told that these fowls were then in the basement of an unoccupied house, into which the urban poulterer had found some way of gaining en-trance. This house, as it happened, was in the street along which we were walking; and the illicit poulterer had been seen to enter a few moments before. The officer accordingly suggested that we go to the front window and flash the light and pho-tograph the man and his poultry at the very mo-ment when the policeman should present himself.

Mr. Brackett fell in with this suggestion. When we came to the house, which was dark and appar-ently uninhabited, the policeman left us and went back to the rear door. He told us that he would

peer into the rear windows with his dark lantern;
then the man with his hens would take refuge in the
front room, where we could get a most unexpected
and amusing picture.

And so it was. When we heard the officer's sig-
nal, a low whistle, Mr. Brackett exploded a cap on
the illuminating powder, and I operated the camera.
In the flash we saw the figure of a man crouching
amid a room full of roosting fowls, which seemed
much disturbed by the sudden radiance. When the
policeman joined us he insisted on a full description of the scene, laughing heartily at the strange
exhibition. He was so desirous to see such a sight
for himself that he gave up his intention of arrest-
ing the violator of the law then and there. The
patrolman expressed a preference for a promenade
with us, stating that he knew where the man lived,
and that he could arrest the fellow whenever he
chose, whereas he might not again have an opportunity to see the workings of the so-called "detective camera." As he walked along with us he suggested various places where we would certainly be
able to get photographs such as we sought. And
to these places we went with him, but without finding anything worthy of reproduction.

At last, after we had wasted two hours or more

in these fruitless wanderings, the storm, which had held off all the evening, broke suddenly. I declared my intention of returning home at once. But the policeman pleaded so pathetically with me to make one more attempt that I yielded. He said he could take us to a bar-room where the business of liquor-selling was carried on all night, in spite of the fact that a renewal of its license had been refused. It was then long past midnight, but the saloon would surely be full of customers, so the officer said, and he offered to take us there, shrewdly surmising that when he was seen there would be a stampede, which we could photograph "on the wing," as he graphically described it.

To this illicit bar-room we went—it seems to have been our fate to be witnesses only of illegal actions. The policeman gave a curious knock at the door, which was immediately opened from within. He instantly pressed forward, and we followed him, ready to take advantage of the occasion. As soon as the bar-tender caught sight of the blue coat of the officer of the law he pulled a cord and put out the gas, hoping to allow his customers to escape under cover of the darkness. But he reckoned without us. Mr. Brackett again flashed the light, and I touched the spring of the camera, and we fixed in black and white the strange scene of hurrying confusion which was revealed to us in the momentary illumination of the premises. This time the policeman was an actual spectator, and his enjoyment of the spectacle was extreme. But it did not interfere with his prompt arrest of the proprietor of the saloon, the only person left in it when the gas was again lighted. Then he notified us that we should have to appear as witnesses against the prisoner.

I hastened to protest, and Mr. Brackett added his arguments to mine. In the end we prevailed, and then we withdrew at once. Mr. Brackett wished to make another attempt, declaring that two photographs were but a meagre result of our night's labors. But I was obdurate. I felt that it was high time we had both retired. I refused absolutely.

We returned home, and I agreed with Mr. Brackett that we should go out again last night. He had an engagement which would keep him down-town until nearly eight o'clock, but he promised to meet me at the South Ferry station of the elevated railroad at nine. We had decided next to attempt the lower end of the city as a more promising field for our investigations.

Yesterday evening, then, a little before eight

o'clock, I set forth to keep my appointment. I
told the waitress, Katey Maloney, not to lock up
the house, as I did not know when I should return;
for of course I could not foresee the impending outrage of which I was to be the innocent victim.

As I was descending the steps of the house I
heard the shrill whistle of the letter-carrier on his
last round. It recalled to me that the necessities
of the rapidly-increasing circulation of *Youth* are
forcing us to go to press earlier and earlier every
month, and that although it is now only November,
yet in a very few weeks we shall be making up the
February number—the Valentine Extra. I remembered that a picture of a postman delivering a letter
would be a most appropriate illustration for that
number of our magazine, and it struck me that I
had now a most excellent oportunity for procuring
such a picture, " taken from life," in the exact sense
of the words, and with the free movement of an unconscious subject.

I crossed the street and turned to face the door
of our house. Suddenly a man whom I did not
recognize as an inmate of the house ran rapidly up
the steps and concealed himself in the vestibule,
having made no effort to ring the bell. As the letter-carrier ascended the steps, with some envelopes

14

in his hand, this strange man came out on the top of the stoop, as though he lived in the house, and extended his hand for the letters.

This struck me as a very strange proceeding. I had already adjusted the apparatus and prepared the powder. I seized the moment when the stranger and the postman were facing each other, with out-stretched hands, to flash the light and fix their image in this attitude on the sensitive plate in the camera.

As the blinding brilliance of the illuminating powder faded away, the darkening dusk descended again, and I was not able to see distinctly what happened. But I am informed that the man who had secreted himself in the vestibule of our house thrust the letter-carrier to one side violently, and sprang down the steps of the stoop and rushed across the street to the spot where I was standing.

The first intimation I had of his presence was a brutal blow on the ear, which almost stunned me. Then the camera was snatched from my hands and smashed against the pavement. A second blow back of my ear knocked off my spectacles, which fell to the ground and were broken. I was severely bruised, and by the suddenness of the attack I was taken unprepared, and altogether very rudely handled, the man remarking in his barbarous vernacular that "he would larn me to print him unbeknownst."

This is an exact and precise statement of all the circumstances connected with the unprovoked and dastardly assault committed on me yesterday evening by the brutal ruffian who is now in custody, and whose name, I am told, is Tim Dwyer. It will be seen that there is no foundation for his allegation that I had been pursuing and persecuting him. I had done nothing of the kind. I had never even heard his name. I had never seen him, so far as I know. I had not injured him in any way. Under these circumstances I deem it my duty to demand the uttermost penalty of the law for his outrageous assault

II.

THE STATEMENT OF MR. TIMOTHY DWYER.

Dictated to a Stenographer by Advice of his Counsel.

I always was counted a paceable, aisy-goin' man, an' there isn't a black dhrop in me veins, nor niver was, an' all I'm sayin' here to-day is thruc, an' nothin' less, be vartue o' me oath. An' whin I tell ye what that fluffy-faced, kitten-headed omadhawn done to me ye'll wonder that I left a whole bone in his body, an' more be token I wouldn't, if I hadn't a heart in me as soft as the belly of a eel.

It goes widout sayin' that whin there's a ruction the man in the check jumper'll be in the wrong of it, whin the man in the tall hat an' specs is as inno-cent as an onconfessed angel—at laste that's always the way of it when the cops take a hand, an' that's why I'm on me defince now, whin av I'd ha' done as I'd a right, I'd ha' bruk his neck wid the first skelp, an' then divil a word he'd ha' let on about the matther at all at all.

To begin wid the beginnin'—an' they say that's the best way whin ye have a long story to tell —I've bin kapein' company off an' on for two year wid Kitty Maloney, her brother bein' an ould towny o' mine, an' the girl herself a dacent slip enough, wid an eye like a young cowlt an' plinty to say for herself. We niver had no cross nor quarrel all the time we were coortin' exceptin' the thrubble the widdy Rooney med, an' sure wanst I got a quiet minnit wid Kitty an' put the commether on her, she niver would belave that the wind o' the word iver passed betune mesilf an' the widdy, an' she doesn't belave it till this day. Not but what the widdy's a gallus piece in her own way, but she's not in the same strate wid Kitty—no, an' I'm saying it on oath, not widin a thousand mile o' her.

But, as I was sayin', there niver was the cross look betune Kitty an' mesilf, barrin' the contimptuous little ruction the widdy riz, an' I was workin' hard an' doin' fine gettin' ready for the day whin I'd haul the colleen home, whin this thrubble kem on me, an' divil resave the minnit's pace or quiet I've had since..

I had bin out in the counthry a little step—at a beootiful place up the Hudson River, where I've a brother o' mine boordin'. His work does be very confinin', poor fellow, an' whin I want to see him I have to go visit him. Well, that's neither here nor there. It was middlin' late whin I got home, an' afore I retired I thought it well to look at me chickens, for I'd bin away all the evenin', an' there's a gang o' coons beyant the Bullyvard 'ud smell a growin' feather quicker nor you cud ha' singed wan. By rason o' the onnayborliness o' me naybors I've been kapein' the chickens undher the cellar o' a house I've taken charge of. They complained o' me— that is, the naybors did, not the chickens—by rason o' the roosters crowin' in the mornin', which is nothin' more nor the nature o' the baste, an' what's to be expected of every dacent fowl. Be that as it may, I had to sing small an' kape the crathurs packed away in a dark basement, wid a careful eye out all the while for Dutch Peter the cop, who niver was known to ax to stir a burglar or a goat or anny other dangerous baste, but he's a howly terror on fowls.

Well, I went in an' counted the hens as well as I cud in the dark, an' the crathurs just sat there an' clucked fair an' aisy, as much as to say, " Tim, *ma bouchla*, niver fear we'll raise no row to get ye into thrubble." It was late annyway, as I sed. Well, all of a suddint come the screech of a whistel let off so clost to me that it med me jump three fut in the air, an' wid that a flash o' light that almost tuk the

sight from me eyes. Well, I was that scared I
didn't know which way to luk, an' it was a good
piece afore I cud be sure I wasn't shot, for the flash
was like a pistol. But a thunderin' big rooster,
worse scared nor I was, tuk me a clout on the side
o' the head that brought me back to me wits again,
for ye see the crathurs were that put about be the
suddint light that they were back an' forwards like
divils. I med out o' that as hard as I cud pelt, an'
it was the mercy o' Providence I thought o' the
coons an' locked the dure afther me.

Now ye'll say that was a middlin' quare thing to
happen to a dacent man, an' he comin' back from
Sing Sing, but that wasn't only the beginnin' of it.
If it had bin a will-o'-the-wisp, an' I'd ha' bin an
acre o' bog, that little light, bad cess to it! cudn't
ha' bothered me more. Afther I'd got out o' the
place an' left the chickens to get over their fright
the best way they cud, what was the nixt most
nateral thing for a man to do undher them sarcum-
stances? Wid the heart put clane acrost in me, an'
the sowls o' me feet an' the palms o' me hands as
cowld as Christmas Eve, there was nothin' to be
done but the wan thing. I didn't know of anny
place I cud get it nigher at hand nor Barney's, on
the corner, for it was gettin' purty late, an' anny

wan that had a license or a character to lose was in
bed long ago.   But divil a hair did Barney care for
character, an' the license he had was no good annyhow.

Kitty's wan o' Father Mathew's girls, an' hates
a glass o' whiskey worse nor she does a Protestant,
but sure I'm not tellin' Kitty all I do, an' av I did
she wouldn't belave it.   An' as for the pledge I tuk
to plaze her, why, the good intintion is everything,
as Father Brennen says, an' sure my intintions is
always good, av I only have the luck to stick to them.

There was a purty middlin' crowd in Barney's an'
Billy Power wanted to hear all the latest news
about me brother Paudeen.   I dun know if I min-
tioned that Paudeen was in thrubble by rason of
an unfortinate accident that happened him awhile
ago, whin a gintleman's watch-chain got twisted
round me brother's slave-button some way.   I niver
got the rights o' the story, an' the cops, who always
belave the worst of a man, med out that it was
stalin' it he was.   They tuk his fortygraft, an' there
niver was a Dwyer so disgraced since me father,
rest his sowl, was thransported for shape-stalin';
but sure that's an honorable perfession over there,
as ye'd know if ye knew annything about the ould
counthry.

Well, to come back to me dhrink! Billy Power was thratin', like a dacent gintleman he is, an' I had me elbow, as it might be, half-ways crooked, an' the glass on a level wid the top button o' me vest, when—whirrush! in runs a cop. Dutch Peter himself, divil a less; an' such a surprise ye niver seen in yer life. Men duckin' an' duckin' for a place 'to hide, an' good liquor left standin' on the bar as if it was as common as muddy wather in Ballinasloe Fair. I had me prisince o' mind, for I was up to Barney's thricks, an' sure enough, afore ye cud say " Howly Moses," he chucked a string he has behind his bar, that works some yoke to the gas fixtures, an' out goes the light, an' there we are. As I sed, I was lookin' out for that, an' I hadn't let go me howlt of me dhrop o' dhrink, so I was just takin' it down fair an' aisy, whin may I niver ate another bit if that same flash didn't ketch me square betune the eyes an' mostly blind me. I had sinse enough to swally down the whiskey wid it all, an' that gimme courage to look, an' I seen the yoke they were shootin' at me; not like anny pistol ever I seen, but more like a tin canister nor that, av ye cud fancy a tin canister loaded up wid blazes instead o' biskit.

Now there were no hens there at all at all. It

was mesilf they were aimin' at, an' if they were goin' to folly me about all over the town wid their ould tin canister an' pelt me whiniver they seen me, I'd put it to anny rasonable man if I'd have e'er a bit o' comfort out o' me life at all.

I got out o' that place purty quick, an' I didn't stop to see if Barney was arristed this time, but it's apt he was, for the place was closed whin I got back, an' Barney does be most ginerally arristed the latther part o' the wake. Some people have the hoight o' rispict for Barney, but more doesn't like a bone in his skin. If it wasn't for the pull he has, I think they'd hang him—divil a doubt o' it.

But av this is to be a statement o' why I fetched young fluffy-face a clout on the lug, I dun know if Barney has much to do wid it. Afther lavin' the saloon I hung around the best part o' the night, an' in the mornin' I tuk a turn down as far as Nineteenth Strate. The mornin's an iligant hour for meditation av ye're disturbed in mind, an' the sarvant-girls do be shakin' out the dure-mats along about the same time. Kitty Maloney works in a boordin'-house, an' I've no doubt does it well, for she's a raal sinsible slip. Well, sure enough, whin I come round the corner who should I see but Kitty, lookin' mighty plazed at the sight o' me, an' beckonin' me wid her dure-mat the same as if it was the flag of ould Ireland.

"Good-mornin', Tim," sez she.

"An' the top o' the mornin' to yersilf, Kitty," sez I.

"An' thin what ails ye?" sez she. "Is it a ghost ye've seen, or what, you look that white?"

"Kitty," sez I, "there's no tellin' what I've seen; but down on yer bended knees an' be thankful ye see me on two feet this day, for it's shot an' wounded I've been."

"Is it shot?" sez she.

"Divil a less," sez I, "for I seen the flash, an' I've that confusion of intillict that they all do have from a wound in the head."

Wid that she began to laugh, an' said it was what I'd been drinkin'; but I towld her that I was a total abstainence son of Father Mathew, an' that no wan knew that betther nor she did, for she'd druv me to sign the pledge hersilf. An' then I up an' towld her all about the tin canister an' the fire flashes.

She didn't take much stock in it. Wimmin is quare annyhow, an' I've seen her take on worse over a little shtroke of a shillalah acrost me head nor she did over all the dangers I'd bin through.

But she had her own talk to let out that mornin', for she was just leppin to go to the Shamrock ball that night, an' she was bound that I should take her.

"Wid a heart an' a half, Kitty," sez I; for she was a very presintible young woman entirely to take to the like; "wid all me heart. But sure what will the ould woman say?"

That was the ould girl that run that hashery, an' she always had a lick o' the rough side of her tongue for me whiniver she seen me.

"Lave me alone," sez Kitty; "sure me aunt in Brooklyn isn't dead yet."

"Begorra she must be the tough ould shtrap, thin," sez I; for more be token she'd been an' pled that aunt to her misthress ivery time she wanted to get out wid me for a year or more.

An' wid that we settled it, not forgettin' a taste of a kiss to kape us good-timpered; an' sure where's the harm in the like, whin there's not a sowl, barrin' a milk wagon, on the block?

Kitty got her lave fast enough to go to her poor sick aunt, an' was waitin' for me below the grocery. Relations is a great convanience av ye use them right.

Well, be the time we'd been at the Shamrock a

couple o' hours, an' had welted the flure middlin'
lively, accordin' as we cud humor the chune o'
the band, there was no gayer lad nor mesilf in North
Ameriky, an' I'd clane forgotten to think o' the tin
canister all the avenin'; though I cudn't get out o'
the notion that the fellow meant me some divilment
yet, an' maybe 'ud chance to howld the yoke a
thrifle straighter nixt time he seen me.

I was givin' Kitty a taste o' refrishments—divil a
much betther it was nor butthermilk—whin who
should come in an' stand right foreninst us but the
widdy Rooney. She had mischief in her eye, an' I
knew she was up to some thavin' thrick whin she
spoke so swate to Kitty.

"Good-avenin', Miss Maloney. Ye're havin' an
iligant dance, I thrust," sez she.

"I can't deny it," sez Kitty, very brisk an' spirited.
"The same to yersilf, ma'am, an' many o' them."

So they went at it hammer an' tongs, the way
two wimmen will do whin they can't talk too much
blarney an' wish too much harm to wan another,
an' these two was so mortial handy at it that I'd as
lief thry an' kape the pace betune a bull an' a holly
bush.

At last the widdy turns to me, an' sez, sez she,
"A word wid ye, Mr. Dwyer, av ye plaze."

" Sartinly, ma'am," sez I, " wid all the pleasure in life," though it's ould Nick himself I'd rather be goostherin' wid that minnit.

" I'm goin' to write to Miss Canby to-morrow," sez she. Miss Canby's the ould maid that kapes the boordin'-house where Kitty works. " I'm goin' to write to Miss Canby, an' let her know what a mighty plisint avenin' our frinds are havin' here."

" An' for what would ye do the like o' that, ma'am ? " sez I, the same as av I didn't know it was for spite.

" For fun an' for fancy," sez she, an' she laughed that plazed that I knew she'd do it, an' av it had ha' bin annywhere else but in a mighty silict ball, I think I'd ha' twisted her neck. " For fun an' for fancy, an' just to aise folks' minds in regard to the health of that very respectable woman Miss Ma- loney's aunt in Brooklyn beyant."

Wid that she went off sniggerin' an' titterin', as if she'd said somethin' very smart, an' I went back to Kitty.

But girls, the best o' thim, is little betther off nor hens in the matther o' sinse, an' she was that mad, or purtended to be, becase I spoke to the widdy, that I had to waste the best part o' an hour an' sivin dances thryin' to soothe her. The colleen

was scared enough, all the same, whin I did get
tellin' her.

"Is it write to Miss Canby?" she sez, all of a
thrimble.

"Divil a less," sez I, thryin' to give it her so I
wouldn't frighten her.

"Och, millia murther! she'll turn me out," sez
she, "widout as much of a character as 'ud make a
pair o' blankets for a flea."

"Suppose she does itself?" sez I; but I knew all
the time that Kitty set great shtore be her situation;
though I wouldn't ha' given a nickel for a dozen o'
them.

"She must be stopped from writin'," sez she.

"Kitty, me darlint," sez I, "av ye had as much
experience wid widdies as I've had, ye'd know that
the divil himsilf cudn't do that."

"Well, av we cud get howlt o' the letther," sez she.

"That might be done," sez I. "I'll hang
around whin the postman comes to-morrow."

"An' what'll ye say to him whin ye seen him,
avick?" sez she.

"Lave that to me," sez I. "Av that limb of a
widdy writes to Miss Canby, she'll do it to-morrow;
an' I'll hang around an' watch close for the letther,
an' let you do the same."

"Ye know the widdy's writin', I suppose, Tim?" sez she, so innocent an' onconcerned like that I slaps out wid, "To be sure; why not?" widout thinkin'. An' mortial sorry I was whin she sez, "Ho! ho!" sez she. "So you've been resavin' letthers from the widdy, have ye?"

"Niver think it, acushla," sez I. "But sure ivery-body ud know a widdy's letther."

"An' how wud they do that?" sez she.

"Becase a widdy always writes wid red ink, as is well known. They dar'n't write wid black ink for fear folks ud think they was mournin' too much afther the first husband, an' that ud spoil the new market."

It tuk time an' a good dale o' solid, sinsible talk to mek her belave that; but I got her home quiet an' aisy afther a while.

The next day I dhropped round for a word while the boorders were fillin' up above-stairs—it's always a mighty paceful time in a boordin'-house—an' Miss Kitty towld me a mighty quare thing.

It wasn't about the widdy. She'd done nothin' yit; but I wasn't goin' to thrust her, for Kitty set desprit store about her not writin' to the ould maid. No; it was about another sarcumstance altogether. The girl wint at it this way.

"Tim," sez she, "whin are ye goin' to give me that fortygraft ye promised me?"

"Tare an' ages, Kitty!" sez I, for she was always axin' for the same thing, till she had me wore out; "is it off on that ould tack ye are agen? Sure ye know that I niver had me pictur' tuk, an' niver will."

"An' why not, Tim?" sez she. "Sure I've seen uglier faces nor yours in the shop windies."

"Uglier ye have, I don't doubt," sez I. "But, be this and be that, ye'll niver see moine there. Think o' the disgrace o' the like to a dacent boy!"

"Faith an' I can't see the disgrace," sez she.

"Is it not see it?" sez I. "To be put up there for the polis anny time they want me? No, Kitty; av iver I have the misfortin to kill a man, I'm willin' to suffer for it as becomes a Dwyer; but wan man in wan family is enough to be disgraced that way."

"Ah, sure enough. Ye towld me yer brother was fortygrafted. I wondher how he stud it?" sez she.

"Begorra he stud it rowlin' on the flure," sez I. "That was how he stud it. For there was three men howldin' him; an' a docthor, wid some bowld divil they called Annie Sthetic, all on to him at the wanst, an' sure what cud the poor fellow do?"

15

"Well, Tim," sez Kitty, spakin' middlin' comical, "I'll forgive ye this time; for I have yer pictur', an' an iligant likeness it is." And wid that she showed me, up to me own face an' eyes, a mane little pictur' o' mesilf tuk wid a glass o' liquor at me lips, an' Billy Power alongside o' me, wid his big mouth open an' his ould caubeen on the back o' his head, as nateral as life.

I declare, there was a minnit I didn't know whether I was slapin' or flyin' !

"Well, now, Kitty," sez I, purty soon, "ye can see that's not me wid a whiskey glass, for ye know I niver touch the like."

"It's powerful like ye, Tim," sez she, laughin'.

"Ah, to think o' yer seein' poor Paudeen in his disgrace," sez I, "an' that big-mouthed docthor alongside o' him ! Ah, there's no knowin' where a man'll land whin he begins by havin' his fortygraft tuk."

"Oh, it's yer brother's pictur'," sez she. "He has a great luk o' ye, thin."

"Powerful," sez I; an' that satisfied her, for she had niver seen him; but I had, an' it didn't satisfy me near so good, for Paudeen no more favors me nor a wisp o' straw favors an ould black kettle. It was aisy enough to contint Kitty, for sure there was

the liquor to prove to her it cudn't be me; but I
was bothered intirely, an' felt like the praste that
the girl kissed widout his ever misthrustin' that
she'd done it.

Where in the world cud they have ketched me
to stale a pictur' off o' me, an' I niver guess the
wrong bein' done me?

I looked closter at the fortygraft, an' I seen a thin
edge o' a face wedged in wan corner; nothin' but
the grin on wan lip of it showin'; but I cudn't be
mistook in that grin. It was Barney.

An' wid that the whole thing lepped at me like a
wink, an' I had it. The tin canister an' the flash o'
light an' the whole bedivilment o' the other night
kem to me, an' I seen how I'd bin abused. But I
got off purty aisy, considerin' what determined
vilyans they was; for I looked close at the pictur'
an' divil a sign o' the hens cud I see, good nor bad.

The bell rung while I was talkin' to Kitty, an' she
had to lave me to go crack eggs or the like for the
boorders. If iver I had to take boorders, I'd liefer
feed pigs; they have nothin' to say agin their vic-
tuals, an' they take whativer ye've a mind to give
'em, besides bein' more betther money's worth in
the long run. Annyhow I had to lave suddint that
minnit, for I heerd Miss Canby's v'ice on the shtairs.

I walked up-town fair an' aisy, an' whin I got to the corner o' Sixtieth Strate, who should I see but the widdy Rooney, an' she just dhroppin' a letther into a lamp-post.

"The top o' the mornin' to ye, ma'am," sez I. "It's airly ye are sendin' valentines."

She gev a wicked soort o' a grin. "I like to be in good time, Tim Dwyer," sez she.

Wid that I knew that she had done it, an' that she had bin writin' her lyin' letther to Miss Canby; for I'd liefer she did lie about the colleen itself nor tell the trut', for the trut' may be full as damagin' as a lie, an' it's harder work upsettin' it.

I seen a letther-carrier wid whom I had enough of an acquaintance to wish him the time o' day, an' I towld him I'd just mailed a highly important doccyment to Nineteenth Strate, an' what time wud it be delivered.

"A few minnits afore eight o'clock in the avenin'," sez he; an' wid that I seen how I cud euchre the ould cat, an' sure enough I wud ha' euchred her, an' no wan a haporth the wiser, av it hadn't been for that divil of a flash that kem jist in time to mek all this thrubble.

I was hangin' around the dure of No. 90—that's the house in Nineteenth Strate—a quarter afore

eight, an' Kitty, the crathur, was watchin' me out
o' the front basement, for she's niver so happy as
whin she kin have her eyes on me. It was middlin'
dark whin the postman kem around; I cud hear his
whistle, an' I run up an' hid jist inside the front
dure. Well, I stipped out to mate him as bowld as
brass, the same as av I owned the block, an' he
handed me three or four letthers all in a bunch.

Did anny wan iver hear tell o' the like? A lone
woman widout a man to her name gettin' all them
letthers at a lick, the same as if she was the Prisi-
dint, jist a purpose to confuse me! I was consid-
therin' that I'd betther tear them all up, for thin
I'd be sure o' the widdy's letther annyhow, whin,
bang! may I niver ate another bit av some one
didn't shoot me from right acrost the strate. Yis,
sir; there it was; the same ould flash leppin up, an'
the same ould tin canister, only this time I wasn't
scared so much as I was mad. I seen the whole
thrick. This fellow was follyin' me round stalin'
pictur's o' me. Very apt he had me likeness among
all the chickens, or he'd given it to Dutch Peter as
ividence agin me, an' I knew he had me cot drinkin'
whiskey afther hours. But this time I was breakin'
no law, only puttin' a stop to mischeevious letthers,
so I didn't give a traunteen fer him. I jist tuk a

flyin' lape down out o' the shtoop, an' I was acrost the strate afore ye cud say whillaloo.

Be vartue o' me oath, I only hot him the three licks—wan to knock him down, wan to sthraighthen him up whin he was fallin', an wan more to lay him down steady an' quiet while I smashed the murtherin' ingine he had; an' av I left a bit o' that bigger nor a bit o' wood, I'm willin' to go to jail fer it. I niver hot him but the three blows, an' he'd bin parse-cutin' o' me fer nights. Av I'd bin a man o' violent timper there's no sayin' but I might ha' hurt him, but there was no satisfaction in b'atin' the like. He was shuk wid the first lick, an' all ran together like a spoonful o' milk curd, squealin' for all the world like a shot hare. They tell me I blacked his eyes an' lift a singin' in his ears he mayn't git over in a month. A black eye! That's a purty thing to mek a fuss about. I've known dacent boys ud be ashamed to be seen goin' home from a dance or a wake widout a pair o' thim. An' as for his ears— bad cess to them—it's little enough alongside o' my character disgraced be his fortygraftin'.

That's all I have to say, an' is a thrue statement o' why I bruk his infernal yoke an' shtroked his fluffy head fer him. He's tuk me face, that is me own property annyhow, an' lift it lyin' round to disgrace

me, for Kitty towld me she found it in his room
that mornin', for he boords in wid ould Miss Canby.
He's bro't the mowltin' disaise on me fowl by the
scare he gev 'em, an' he cost me tin cints to go to
mass, for I didn't know but what the divil was afther
me, flashin' fire at me in quare places in the dark,
an' in close hoults wid me sowl. If that yoke o'
his iver takes a pictur' agin, it'll be becase the
divil is in it ; an' if anny wan blames me fer what
I've done, all I ax them is to put theirsilves in me
place, an' see how they'd like it thimsilves.

Av ye can square this thing wid the young man,
I'd let him off an' not take the law o' him for felo-
nious fortygrafts ; for Kitty's lost her place wid
Miss Canby, an' we'll git married Sunday very apt
av I don't be locked up for this night's work.

But sure what can they do to me, widout they
mek it out that silf-defince is a crime in New York ?

THREE WISHES,

(In Collaboration with F. Anstey.)

THREE WISHES.

I.

ON the south coast of England, where a white headland juts into the Channel, stands the High-School of Witherington, a new and handsome group of buildings, with a garden before the master's door, and a large play-ground spreading away to the woods which mask the brow of the hill. When the summer sun shines on this play-ground, noisy with boys, it is as pleasant a sight as one could wish to see; but on a dark January afternoon, toward the end of the Christmas vacation, when there are only two lads loitering across its empty expanse, its appearance is less cheerful.

A chill wind was blowing up from the Channel across the Downs, and one of the two boys, a little taller and slighter than his companion, shivered, and buttoned his overcoat.

"This is just the meanest climate I ever saw," he said. "It ain't real winter, with snow and ice so

that a fellow can skate—it's only damp and disagreeable all the time."

"It does snow here sometimes," returned his
companion, a sturdy, thick-set lad of about twelve.
"Wait till you've been here a whole winter and
you'll see."

"It doesn't snow enough to coast, does it?" asked
the taller youth, apparently of about the same
age. "In America a winter is no good unless we
coast."

"What's coasting?" the English boy asked.

"Coasting is sliding down hill," the American
answered, with a glow of enthusiasm. "It's just
bully, I tell you!"

"It sounds rather fun," said Jack Ainsley, the
English boy.

"I wish my folks hadn't had to go to Rome, and
then I shouldn't have had to come here right in the
middle of vacation, when there isn't anybody here
but you."

"You'll like it better when the boys get back,"
Jack replied; "and I'm really worse off than you,
for my people are out in India, and I may not see
them for years yet."

"That is rough on you, I allow," admitted the
American, whose name was Heywood H. Brevoort.

"I had a letter from the mater the day before Christmas, and she said it might be two years before she came home. She said that Colonel Kavanagh, an old friend of hers, was coming up here to see me; but he hasn't been yet."

"But you've friends here and I don't know anybody at all," Heywood responded. "You've been here for a year now, and you know all the other boys when they come back; and you're going to a party this evening."

"I wish you were coming too," said Jack.

"I wish I was, but I don't know the Gowers," replied Heywood. "What I do wish is to be back in America. I'd go coasting all night."

"There isn't any good wishing; you know that won't help you," said the English boy.

"Wishing's lots of fun, anyhow," returned the American. "I like to wish for things, and sometimes I half think I've got 'em, I wish so hard."

"I've longed for a magic lantern," commented Jack, "but it wasn't the same as getting it."

"Those old magicians in the 'Arabian Nights,' you know," Heywood went on, "they had the thing down fine. They had a lamp or a ring or something, and whenever they wanted anything, they just rubbed their old lamp, and a big black spook

came, and they ordered him 'round, and they had
what they wanted in no time."

"Is 'spook' what you call the 'slave of the
lamp?'" asked Jack.

"He's one kind of a spook," replied Heywood.

"I wish we had a lamp of that sort now."

"It would be dead loads of fun, wouldn't it? I'd
keep that black spook on the trot, I tell you! I
wonder if I couldn't make him learn lessons for
me?" said Heywood.

"What would be the use of that?" said Jack;
"*you'd* have to say them, you know."

"I hadn't thought of that," Heywood admitted,
ruefully.

"I shouldn't care so much for the lessons," returned Jack; "but there's ever so many things I'd
like. I'd send him for a magic lantern, for one thing,
and for a bicycle, and for the best stamp collection
in the world, and for a telescope you could tell
the time with on a church clock a hundred miles
away."

"Generally one only has three wishes, you know,"
Heywood remarked in turn. "I'd begin by wishing
to be taken over to America, to coast all this evening, and to go skating to-morrow. I suppose a
Djinn can make it freeze if you order him?"

" I dare say," Jack answered. " I don't know much about Djinns myself."

" I've read enough to know pretty much what they're like," said Heywood. " I guess I'd recognize one if I happened on him."

" Well, I suppose I should too. But what bosh! As if we were *likely* to !"

" Well, I don't know about that. I never heard any reason why there shouldn't be Djinns now just as much as there were in the 'Arabian Nights.' It all depends on your having the right sort of lamp or ring or something or other." And here Heywood sank his voice to a mysterious whisper. " Have you ever tried rubbing a lamp or a ring to see what would happen ?"

" No. Have you ?"

" Lots of times," was the prompt reply.

" And what happened ?"

" Nothing."

" Then what's the good of trying ?" was Jack's natural inquiry.

" Well, I don't give up the idea," answered the American boy. " You can't tell when the right ring or the right lamp may turn up. There isn't any sign by which you can pick 'em out without trying, and if you don't try, you may miss the very lamp which the black spook has to obey. I don't believe in throwing away chances. I've taken a rub on 'most every lamp I ever laid my hands on, and most rings too. You see, even in the 'Arabian Nights' the people didn't generally know that they had the Djinn's lamp. More'n half the time they rubbed it by accident, and then they *were* surprised when the slave of the ring appeared and bowed to the ground, and asked them what they wanted. Oh, I tell you I've been studying this thing up ever since I first got at the 'Arabian Nights,' and sooner or later I may get hold of the right ring."

The English boy listened to this American outburst somewhat doubtfully.

" Have you tried it on your own ring?" he asked at last.

" Pshaw!" answered Heywood, "that ring of mine isn't metal."

" And must it be metal?"

" I think so—leastways I never read about one working satisfactorily that wasn't: generally they are old iron."

" And what is your ring made of?"

" It's an Indian ring --not your Indian, you know, but our Indians, Pawnees or Sioux or Chippewas.

I got it at Niagara. It's made of porcupine quills dyed and twisted together and——"

Here Master Heywood's description of the peculiarities of his ring was suddenly cut short by the sound of carriage wheels approaching the master's entrance.

"There's the Gowers' carriage come for me," cried Jack. "I must be off."

The boys ran together to the front door. As the carriage drove off, Jack thrust his head out of the window and bade his comrade good-by.

"I don't know why a porcupine quill ring shouldn't work just as well as any other, for all it isn't down in the books," thought the American boy as he lingered in the shrubbery of the master's garden. The twilight was beginning to fade away. "I suppose the Djinn of an Indian ring would be a chief of some sort, Red Jacket or Osceola, now. I'd like to see either of 'em, and if they were spooks and had to obey the ring, I don't see but what they'd be just as useful as the other kind."

As these thoughts ran through his mind rapidly, his fingers had closed about the barbarically-colored circlet which adorned his right hand. He was in · the middle of the strip of garden which stretched beside the play-ground when he took a resolution,

16

and he began to rub the ring on his little finger vio
lently with the palm of his left hand.

"It never did any good before," he said to himself, "and I don't know as it'll do any good now,
but I might as well try it on. What should I ask
for if he came? I'd better settle that now. It
wouldn't do to have no commands ready for him;
he'd think I was a fool. I can't make up my mind
what's best here without Ainsley. It wouldn't be
a bad idea if I said in a careless kind of way I
wanted three wishes to start with. That would give
me time to look around and save me the bother of
calling him up. You have to get used to the look
of these fellows."

Suddenly the boy stopped short in fright. As
though the ground had opened to give him passage,
there stood before the lad a strange dark figure of
a man in Oriental garb. The boy stared in silent
astonishment at the mysterious person who towered
above him in the deepening dimness.

After a moment of tension, while Heywood
could hear his heart beating violently, and while his
brain whirled at the sudden fulfilment of his summons, the dark figure took a step forward and
bowed and said, "Sahib."

As the weird messenger advanced toward him the

boy started back, and in the constraint of his move-ment the ring was jerked from his finger and rolled away in the grass. For the moment he did not dare to stoop to recover it.

At last the lad summoned his courage.

"Are you the slave of the ring?" he asked, in a voice which trembled in spite of his utmost endeavor.

"Sahib?" repeated the figure.

"Are you come to do my bidding?" cried the boy, gaining confidence. "Can I have my three wishes?"

The dark figure bowed again and replied: "The young Sahib shall have what he wishes to-morrow."

"Oh," said the boy, "I can have them to-morrow —sure?"

"Yes, Sahib," was the respectful answer. "I come again to-morrow."

"I'd like Jack to have a show in this thing," thought Heywood. So he spoke again: "Look here; I have got a friend here. I suppose it will be the same thing if I let him use one of the wishes?"

"The Sahib's friend can use it, too," was the reply.

"All right." Heywood felt his spirits returning. "I'm to have my three wishes to-morrow, and you'll see that I get 'em—three, you know?"

"There are three—yes, Sahib."

"I am very much obl— No, I mean that will do for the present. You can go back to wherever you came from."

Again the sable figure bowed; then it turned, and to Heywood's startled eyes it seemed to fade into darkness, to melt into thin air.

When he was alone, Heywood looked about him curiously. Then he drew a long breath. Then he gave a whistle of surprise.

"I ain't asleep, am I?" he queried of himself; whereupon he pinched his arm and convinced himself that he was not dreaming.

"He's a useful kind of thing to have about; but he makes me awful creepy at first. I guess I'll get over jumping after a time. It would be fun to rub the ring in class-time and see him come up through the floor. Oh, I mean to be a popular boy in this school—don't I, just?" Here he hugged himself with anticipatory delight.

"And to think I've had that ring all this time and never tried it before—and it was the right kind, after all. I wonder where it's gone to?"

And with this he stooped and began to search in the grass; but the ring was nowhere to be found. The lad looked for it long and diligently, yet in vain. At last he gave over the quest, resolved to resume it in the morning.

He walked from the garden to the play ground, and began to pace to and fro, going over all the incidents of his meeting with the mysterious unknown, and recalling every word of their brief conversation. He doubted whether he had really heard and seen what he had heard and seen. With all his imagination and power of make-believe, he was startled and staggered by this seemingly supernatural response to his summons. He thought the matter over until he did not know what to think.

When he was called, he went in to his supper with his head in a whirl; and a companion, had he had one, could not but have remarked the wandering of his mind.

In time he went up to bed in the huge empty dormitory, which he alone now shared with Jack Ainsley. Although he undressed, he found it impossible to sleep until the return of his friend should permit him to give vent to his emotions, and to impart to another the marvel under which his head was still reeling.

At length Jack Ainsley returned from his tardy Christmas party. It was with difficulty that Heywood restrained himself while he listened to Jack's account of the various delights of the evening's entertainment. That which had most impressed him was the beautiful new tricycle which young Gower had received as a Christmas box from his father.

"That's the kind of present I should like," Jack cried, as he described this machine with glowing enthusiasm, undressing the while and making ready for bed. "If we could only have three wishes—you remember what we were talking about this after-noon? Well, I'd choose a tricycle like Gower's for my first wish."

This was the effective opening for which Hey-wood had been waiting.

"Perhaps I will give you your wish," he said, with dignity.

"You can when your Djinn comes, you know," returned Jack, laughing as he got into bed; "not before."

"Then I can do it now," Heywood replied, sol-emnly and with an unequalled self-satisfaction. "The Djinn has come!"

"Oh, rot!" said Jack, stretching himself out in bed.

"Honest Indian!" cried Heywood, a little taken aback at his friend's stolid reception of his startling news. I mean it! I rubbed the ring, as you said, and the Djinn came."

"What?" almost shouted Jack, sitting bolt up-right in bed.

"I was in the garden just after you went off, and I rubbed the ring and the slave of the ring ap-peared."

"What was he like?"

"He was dressed just as they are in the 'Arabian Nights,' and he had on a turban and——"

"What was *he* like himself?" interrupted Jack.

"Like? Oh, like the ones in the book! He was dark and very tall—immensely tall; he must have been 'most ten feet high, not counting his turban. And his eyes flashed like—like fireworks."

"Did he come out of a column of smoke or with a clap like thunder?" asked Jack.

"There was some smoke," said Heywood; "I won't be certain about the thunder."

"Was he jolly to you?" inquired the English boy.

"I made him know his place pretty soon, I tell you," the American answered. "He salaamed three times, bowing down until his head touched the ground, and then he said, 'I am thy slave and the slave of those who have the ring. Command

and I obey !' I was so surprised that I rubbed the
ring off my finger, and it fell on the grass and rolled
away, and I haven't been able to find it. We must
look in the morning."

"H'm !" said Jack doubtfully. "Why don't you
make the Djinn find it ? "

"How can I ?" Heywood answered. "I can't
call him without the ring ; and even if I should meet
him, I'd never dare tell him I'd lost the ring, because then I shouldn't have any power over him."

"Have you got any power over him now ? " asked
Jack.

"Not over him exactly. You see, it was like
this : I didn't want to be hurried, so my first command was that he should grant me my next three
wishes. And I arranged so you could have one of
them."

"Not really ? " cried Jack. "Thanks, awfully,
Brevoort! You're a trump !"

"We won't hurry over this," said Heywood, who
perhaps had some reluctance to face the spook
again just yet. "I believe in treating your slaves
like human beings. I'll match you who has the
first wish."

"All right," returned Jack, to whom the American boy had explained the mysteries of "matching."

Each lad reached across the bed to his pockets and secured a coin, which he tossed in the air and covered with his left hand as it fell on his right palm.

"I'll match you," said Heywood.

"All right," answered Jack, looking at his coin. "Mine's a head."

"And mine's a tail," Heywood returned; "the first wish is yours."

"I say, Brevoort, do you really believe in this Djinn?" asked Jack doubtfully.

"Of course I do," cried Heywood indignantly. "Didn't I see him, and didn't he give me three wishes, and haven't I let you have the first one?"

"Do you think I'll get it?" was the English boy's next doubtful question.

"Just you wait till to-morrow and see if you don't get it; and if you don't it'll be your own fault for not wishing hard enough."

"All right," said Jack again, with a little more confidence, kindled from his friend's. "I'll wish hard enough if wishing will do it."

"What are you going to wish for?" asked Heywood.

"I'll stick to what I said first—I'll wish for a tricycle like young Gower's. I never saw one I liked better."

"I don't know that I shouldn't go higher than a tricycle," said Heywood doubtfully. "Those 'Arabian Nights' fellows chose more expensive things than that. But come to think of it, we'd better begin gradually, perhaps. When we find the ring we can spread ourselves. Now you must wish hard— real hard."

"I'll wish hard enough, never fear," the English lad replied.

There was silence for a minute or two. It was far later than either of the boys was wont to sit up, and they were both of them getting sleepy despite their unusual experiences.

"Are you wishing?" was Heywood's yawning inquiry.

"Yes," Jack answered drowsily.

"Hard?" queried the American.

"Hard as I can," replied the English lad.

In a few seconds more they were both fast asleep.

II.

THE slumber of school-boys is always heavy and hearty, and never more so than in vacation, when there are no sudden bells to arouse them. So it was that both Jack Ainsley and Heywood Brevoort overslept themselves on the morning after the former had been to the Gowers' party and the latter had rubbed his Indian ring. When they were awakened, it was Heywood who managed to dress first. He descended from the dormitory as speedily as he could. After a good night's sleep, he did not know what to think of his adventure of the preceding evening. In the chill morning he felt doubts which he would have denied the night before while talking to Ainsley. Whom had he seen? And what was it that this strange messenger had really said to him? These were questions to which he could return no satisfactory answer. If the wish had been fulfilled in any way, Heywood's confidence would have been amply restored; and when first he waked he had cast a doubtful glance about the dormitory, half hoping that he might see the tricycle by the side of his friend's bed.

As he drew near to the housekeeper's room, where he and Jack took their meals in lonely state during the holidays, the parlor-maid met him and said: "Isn't Master Ainsley down yet? There's something come for him."

"Where? What is it?" cried the American boy, with a sudden revulsion of hope.

"It's in the hall by the door," she answered; "it's a wheel thing."

"Jack, come and see!" he cried, as he caught sight of his friend at the foot of the stairs. "There's something for you!"

"What is it?" shouted Jack, springing along after him.

As they came to the end of the hall, there stood a brand-new tricycle.

"Didn't I tell you?" cried Heywood. "*Now* what do you say? Look at your name on the label. Do you think I'm selling you now?"

"I never did think that exactly," Ainsley answered; "only—it all seems so queer, don't it? To have my wish granted so soon!"

Then examining the tricycle more particularly, he added: "I say, this isn't just like Gower's, you know!"

"Isn't it?" asked the American, a little annoyed

at this caviling. "That's your own fault, then. You should have wished harder and plainer. How's a Djinn to know one tricycle from another? Some Djinns would have brought a perambulator."

The parlor-maid came down the hall to tell them that breakfast was ready.

"I say, Mary," cried Jack, still doubting, despite the tangible evidence before him, "where did this tricycle come from?"

"It was brought here this morning by a black man," was the answer.

Jack and Heywood looked at each other, and whatever of suspicion they may have retained now faded away.

"Was he a very tall man, Mary?" asked Heywood.

"Uncommon tall, and very dark," she replied.

"And did he wear a turban?" the American inquired again.

"Yes," she returned; "but your breakfast will be cold if you don't come now."

As she left them, Heywood looked across to Ainsley with a smile of triumph. "That's him!" he said.

After breakfast the two boys sought diligently for the Indian ring. Heywood was not able to iden-tify with certainty the exact spot where he had stood when the black man appeared before him; and this was perhaps the reason why their search was unavailing. It seemed to them that they had examined every inch of the strip of garden; but they failed to discover the missing ring.

They spent nearly an hour in the search, the tricycle standing the while by the steps.

"I say, Brevoort," said Ainsley at last, straightening up with an effort, "let's give up the ring for this morning; we can look again to-morrow. It must be somewhere, you know, and we are bound to find it."

"I don't see where the pesky thing can have got to!" Heywood remarked, in disgust.

"My back is nearly broke stooping over, and I'm going to rest it by a turn on the tricycle. Come along."

They took the machine out into the road, and Ainsley mounted and started it gently. A hundred yards from the gate the road dropped away abruptly, and there was a sharp descent. At the top of this the English boy drew up.

"We'd better not try the hill, I think," he said, "until we can work this thing. You ride it back."

Heywood took Jack's place, and rode the tricycle up to the gate and beyond, his friend following on

foot. When they were abreast of the house, the
parlor-maid came out and called the English boy.

"Master Ainsley, there's a gentleman to see
you."

"It's Colonel Kavanagh, I'm sure," cried Jack.
"I say, Brevoort, come right up to the house; I
want to show him my tricycle!"

On the steps of the school stood a handsome,
soldierly man, with a pleasant smile and laughing
eyes.

"And this is Jack Ainsley?" he said, as the boy
came up. "I should have known you anywhere—
you favor your mother. I am Colonel Kavanagh,
and I'm an old friend of your mother's. I saw her
in India not two months ago, and I promised her
to give her boy a look-up."

"I had a letter from the mater last week," Jack
replied, "and she told me you were coming down
to see me."

"She's well, I trust?" Colonel Kavanagh inquired.

"The mater? Oh, she's well," the boy answered,
with his eyes fixed on the movements of Heywood
Brevoort, who was manœuvring the tricycle. The
officer followed the direction of the boy's glance.

"I see you've got your tricycle," he said.

"I got it only this morning," Jack replied. Then,

lowering his voice, he pursued: " Do you believe in
magic ?"

" In what ?" queried the colonel, with a faint smile.

" In magic ?—in Djinns, like in the 'Arabian
Nights,' you know ?"

" I don't know," the colonel answered; " I never
met a Djinn; have you ?"

" I haven't, but Brevoort has."

" Oh," said Colonel Kavanagh gravely. " Brevoort has seen a Djinn ? And who is Brevoort ?"

" That's Brevoort there, on the tricycle. He's an
American boy, and he has an Indian ring; at least
he had, but he's lost it; and he rubbed it and the
slave of the ring appeared and said he could have
three wishes, and we tossed who should have the
first, and I won, and I wished for a tricycle, and
this morning here it was."

" So that's the way you got it, is it ?" asked
Colonel Kavanagh. " It must be very convenient to
be able to get things by wishing for them. And
Brevoort really saw a Djinn, eh ? I'd like to hear
all about it."

" I'll call him over—he won't mind," said Jack.
" Here, Brevoort, I say !"

The American boy dismounted from the machine
and came towards them.

"This is my friend Brevoort, Colonel Kavanagh," said Jack, by way of introduction.

"Glad to see you, sir," said Heywood, holding out his hand. "My father was a colonel in the war. He was wounded at Seven Pines."

"Ainsley tells me that you have seen a Djinn," the colonel began, frankly. "I'm interested in Djinns, and I'd like to hear all about it."

Heywood blushed suddenly, and his cheeks tingled while he was telling his tale.

"I don't know much about Djinns except what I've read; and I've only seen one, and him only once, so far, and it was getting dark, too."

"I've never seen even one," said Colonel Kavanagh. "Where did you meet him?"

"Out there in the bit of garden by the playground. You see, I've got an Indian ring made of porcupine quills, and I'd tried rubbing all sorts of rings to call up a Djinn, and they never came, and Jack here said why didn't I try this Indian ring, and so I did, last evening, out there, and I rubbed, and rubbed, and suddenly a great tall black man rose up before me and bowed——"

"Ah," remarked the colonel, with interest, "I see—it was there that you met the Djinn. And what time was this?"

17

" About five o'clock last evening."

" And he was a tall, black man, with dark clothes and a high turban——"

" Have you seen him too ? " interrupted Brevoort.

" I regret to say that I have not yet met a Djinn face to face," replied the colonel, smiling.

" Then how did you know how he looked ? " asked the American boy.

" How did I know ? " repeated Colonel Kavanagh ; " why, I know how a respectable Djinn ought to be clothed. Did I describe the dress of the one you saw ? "

" Exactly," Heywood answered.

" That is a little curious, isn't it ? " said the colonel. " And he gave you three wishes ? "

" Well, I asked him if I could have three wishes, and he said I could, in the morning. So Jack and I matched to see who should have the first wish, and he won, and he wished for a tricycle. I don't think he quite believed in my Djinn, but when he came down-stairs this morning and found that tricycle, and heard Mary say it had been brought by a big black man, why, naturally, that just staggered him."

" Yes," said Colonel Kavanagh, " I can see that

it would stagger him. I confess that it staggers me. I can hardly help believing that your Djinn had something to do with it."

"I believe it now, of course. I didn't at first," said Jack. "Still it is rather extraordinary, isn't it ? "

"Yes," said Colonel Kavanagh again. "It is extraordinary. In fact, I don't mind telling you that it is one of the most extraordinary things I ever heard of." He paused and then looked at Heywood. "It's a pity you lost that ring. If you had it I should ask you to call up that Djinn again. I'm very anxious to get a good look at him."

"I don't think he'd like to be called just to be made a show of," said Heywood, not quite ingenuously. "But I'll see how he feels about it when we find the ring. We're going to look for it again and again till we do."

"They tell me that the doctor has gone up to London and will not return until to-morrow afternoon, so I shall come back then to see him," the colonel remarked. "If you have found the ring by that time I wish you would kindly let me know. In the mean while I suppose you will be riding about on the tricycle. Are you not afraid to trust yourself on so ghostly a gift ? "

"The tricycle is all right," Jack spoke up promptly. "I've looked to that. It's come from a first-rate maker. It's one of the best I ever saw."

"Ah," said the colonel meditatively; "and how do you suppose the Djinn got it?"

"Bought and paid for it, I should say," was Jack's answer.

"You don't think the Djinn *stole* it, sir, do you?" asked Heywood.

"No," said Colonel Kavanagh, as he began to walk to the gate—"no, I shouldn't like to believe that the Djinn was dishonest, but I confess I'd like to know just how he came to pick out that particular tricycle."

"He knew a good one, I'm sure," cried Jack.

"It seems to have been selected with care," the colonel remarked. "But if I were you, I don't think I'd risk running down this hill with it you might lose control. I'll see you to-morrow." And with this he nodded to them and passed through the gate.

"Jolly sort of chap, the colonel," commented Jack.

"I wish he wouldn't look as though he wanted to laugh all the time," was Master Brevoort's criticism.

III.

AFTER this interview the boys went out again with the tricycle, which afforded many joys not to be exhausted speedily. They rode it in turn at first and finally together, one working the wheels and the other standing up behind on the rear axle.

For awhile they were content to go to and fro on the more or less level road before the gates of the school, avoiding the declivity against which Colonel Kavanagh had warned them.

But at last, as the muscles of their legs began to tire a little with the unwonted exercise, it struck them that they could ride down the hill without any exertion, and that they could come up again on foot, which would fatigue them less than did the tricycle.

So Jack carefully steered the tricycle into the middle of the road, Brevoort supporting himself on the rear axle as best he could. When they came to the brow of the hill and began to descend towards the town, Ainsley tightened his grip on the brake.

"This is fun!" cried Heywood. "It's almost as good as coasting!"

"If your coasting is any better fun than this, I'd like to have a go at it," Ainsley returned.

The brow of the hill sloped away gently, but the road soon dropped sharply. When the two boys reached this point, the tricycle was going very swiftly.

"I say," cried Jack, "we're going too fast, aren't we?"

"I've coasted down a bigger hill than this lots faster than we are going now," answered the American.

Just here the road dropped away again, and there was again an increase of speed.

"But you can pull up if you like," Heywood added hastily, conscious that their speed was in excess of safety.

"That's all very well," the English boy responded; "but I can't stop now. I've got the brake on, but it won't stop!"

"Look out for the old boy in front there!" shouted Brevoort suddenly.

Ainsley had been giving his attention to the brake, but now he looked up. Right in front of them was an elderly man, rather portly in person.

THREE WISHES.

"Hi, there!" yelled Jack.

"Clear the track!" Heywood cried.

But it was too late. The old gentleman was startled as he heard the cry. Turning, he saw two boys on a tricycle madly descending on him. He lost his head for a moment and hesitated. First he went to the right, and then he went to the left; and then he stepped back and said, "Take care, take care; you'll run over me!"

"Steer to the right!" screamed Brevoort.

The old gentleman's hesitancy had confused Ainsley, who steered to the left and then to the right. Fortunately his steady pressure on the brake had begun to affect their speed, and when at last they came into collision with the old gentleman, the shock was not as violent as it might have been. But it sufficed to upset the tricycle, to spill off Ainsley and Brevoort, and to throw their victim off his feet.

"You are not hurt, are you?" asked Heywood, who was the first to get on his feet; and who went at once to the assistance of the stranger.

"If I've no bones broken, it's no thanks to you," responded the old gentleman angrily.

"We are very sorry," began Ainsley.

"We didn't mean to," were Heywood's first

words, when the old gentleman interrupted them both.

"Of course you didn't mean to," he cried. "If you had meant it, I'd have you locked up in jail! Of course you are sorry; but that wouldn't mend my bones if I'd broken 'em!"

"But you haven't broken any, have you?" Ainsley asked, as he picked up the tricycle.

"What's that to you?" shouted the elderly and irascible person.

"That's so," replied Heywood "You are all right there. *We* don't care whether you break in two!"

"No impudence, you young monkey!" said the old gentleman, with increasing wrath.

"Gorilla yourself!" was Heywood's retort.

"What?" shouted the stranger. "Do you mean to bandy words with me?" And here he flourished menacingly his heavy cane with a shining silver knob at the top.

"Oh, come. off!" answered the American boy; "you began it—you called us monkeys!"

"Things have come to a pretty pass in this country, if a man cannot go out of town for a day on business without being exposed to assault and insult from a band of young ruffians."

"Oh, I say now," interrupted Ainsley; "we are not young ruffians."

"I suppose you two young rascals belong to that school on the hill there?" inquired the old gentleman.

"Yes, we do," answered Ainsley.

"And what of it?" was Brevoort's question.

"I'll make it my business to call on the master and ask him why he doesn't teach you young cubs better manners."

"I'd sooner be a young cub than an old bear, any day!" responded Brevoort promptly.

"Now mark my words," said the old gentleman, mastering his anger, and speaking with much force; "mark my words! I believe that you two boys took a wanton pleasure in running into me. I believe that you did this on purpose. As you have seen fit to add insult to injury, I shall state my belief to your master. I had intended to return to town by the five-o'clock train, and I may be forced to do so; but if it is possible, I shall present myself at the school this afternoon, on my way back to the station. Then we shall see what your master has to say to your impudence and your brutality. Now, no more words. You may save your breath to defend yourself to the master."

And so saying, the old gentleman turned away from them and resumed his descent of the hill.

Heywood was about to throw a few words of defiance after the departing enemy, when Jack checked him.

"Let him go," he said; "we needn't make things any worse than they are."

And with that he began to push the tricycle slowly up the hill.

Warmed with the combat, Heywood was full of fight, and it was a few minutes before he saw the gravity of their situation.

They returned in silence, crest-fallen and conscious of their wrong-doing. Perhaps it was this which made them not a little irritable with themselves and with each other.

When they came to the brow of the hill and the more level road lay before them, Heywood mounted the tricycle and Jack walked by his side, still deep in thought.

"I *knew* something would come of getting a machine through a Djinn!" said Jack, at last, lugubriously.

"The machine's well enough!" retorted Brevoort, promptly defending his Djinn. "Don't blame the Djinn because you can't steer. If you had turned the handles the way I told you, we shouldn't have run over him!"

"Well, it's no good talking about that now—it's done, and there's an end of it!"

"Do you think he. meant what he said about coming up to the school this evening and complaining?"

"I dare say. He'd have been all right if you hadn't cheeked him like that."

"Make out it's my fault! I wasn't going to stand there as calm as a clam while he was calling names. I guess he knew my opinion of him by the time I was through."

"You made it ten times worse by going and slanging him like that."

"I didn't, so now!"

"You did, so there! You think yourself so jolly sharp."

"Well, I'd be sorry if I wasn't sharper than some folks," said the American sulkily.

"All right," retorted Jack; "if that's the way you're going to talk, I'll trouble you to get off that tricycle—it's mine!"

"That's pretty mean—considering. If it wasn't for me you wouldn't have had a tricycle to order me off. Here, *take* your old tricycle. I'm sorry I gave you one of my wishes now, if this is all the gratitude I get!"

Jack was ashamed and penitent in a moment.

" No, I say, Brevoort; I wasn't in earnest then," he said; "don't get off. It's all rot our quarrelling like this. We're both in the same mess. Do you think he was only pretending to be in a bait?"

" We ran over his toes and took him full in the waistcoat—he looked as though he was pretty mad," said Heywood pensively. "And he knows we be-long to the school here. He'll come—if he has to drop everything to do it. There's only one chance for us."

" What's that?"

" Why, you heard him say he had come down here for the day, and he thought it hard he couldn't be safe in a place like this?"

" But he said he'd come as soon as he had fin-ished his business here—on his way back to the station. He's got lots of time between this and evening."

" *Let* him come!" said Brevoort; "he'll only find the housekeeper—the doctor doesn't come back till to-morrow."

" No more he does—hooray!" cried Jack; "then we're all right. Mrs. Cossett won't speak, I know."

So they reached the school in an easier state of mind.

However, after the mid-day dinner, Jack, who had been prowling about alone, came with a long face into the school-room, where Brevoort was sitting.

"I say," he began, "I just found Mary lighting the doctor's fire, and I got out of her that he's sent a telegram to say he'll be here by the three-o'clock train this afternoon."

"Then we're treed!" was Heywood's comment; "for that old chap will turn up sure as fate, and now, if he does come, the doctor will be in. Is he strict?"

"Rather, in some things."

"But, after all, it was an accident."

"That old buffer will swear we did it on purpose; and then," said Jack, "you—we did rather rag him. Yes, the doctor's sure to be awfully shirty. He'll keep us in the play-ground till the fellows come back, and stop tricycling—if he doesn't take it away altogether."

"Then there's an end to our fun!" said Heywood disconsolately. "Perhaps the doctor won't come after all, something may happen to stop him.

"I wish it would!"

"I *say*, Brevoort!" exclaimed Jack.

"Where's the harm in that?"

"Nothing, only he won't come now—that's all."

"Why not?"

"Don't you remember the Djinn? You said you *wished.*"

"Oh, but that don't count. I wasn't really wish-ing, and the Djinn didn't mean that sort of wish," remarked the American boy.

"I don't think that matters. It *was* a wish, and he's bound to grant it. You've used up your second wish."

"That's so," said Heywood thoughtfully. "I don't know, come to think of it, that the case was bad enough to fool away another wish on; but I've done it. The doctor won't come now. That's something, and we can make it up when we find that ring."

"Let's have another hunt for it before it gets too dark," suggested Jack. "If we can get it before the old gentleman comes, you might set your Djinn at him."

"That would be splendid," agreed Heywood; "he'd make the old boy sit up, wouldn't he?"

"You'd have to tell him he mustn't hurt him really, you know," said Jack, "or we should only get into a worse row."

"I'll drop him a hint about that," said the American easily. He was by this time hunting about on the gravel. "But I'm beginning to think we never shall get that ring now."

"Look here, Brevoort, you—you haven't been selling me all this time? It's all right about this Djinn?"

"If it wasn't, how do you account for that tricycle?" demanded Heywood triumphantly.

"I forgot that; but I wish you hadn't lost that ring. Or do you think the Djinn bagged it when you let it drop?"

"If he has, he'll stick to it," said Heywood gloomily; "he's cute enough for that. Then I've lost my Djinn. It's rough having him and losing him like that, all at once."

"You've got one more wish—that's always something," suggested Jack.

"So I have. I'll be real careful about this one. I might wish to have the Djinn back again."

"That wouldn't do," interposed Jack quickly; "because, you see, when he came you wouldn't have the ring and he wouldn't be your slave."

"No more he would. No, I won't risk that, but I might wish to find the ring."

"Not if the Djinn's got it."

"Well, I'll study up what to wish bimeby. Now we've got to try if the ring isn't here after all."

But they searched in vain until the darkness began to gather, and Mrs. Cossett appeared at the school steps.

"Master Ainsley," she called, "will you come here a minute?"

Jack went, and after a short colloquy rejoined his friend.

"We've got to go to the station," he announced shortly; "the doctor hasn't come, and Mother Cossett thinks the train has been delayed somehow; she seems in a funk about something the milkman has told her, and she wants us to go and find out what's up."

"You go," said Heywood; "I feel like finding that ring."

"No, come with me, I'd rather," urged Jack, who did not seem to care about his own company just then. Brevoort yielded, seeing that it was really too dark to admit of any prospect of finding the ring till daylight.

There was a larger crowd than usual at the station; the men lounging about the station-yard seemed to be discussing something with an excitement very different from their customary lassitude;

on the platform, groups still more excited were collected; and all officials, from the station-master down to the paper-boy, were being eagerly applied to for information. Jack and Heywood stood endeavoring to discover the reason of this unwonted stir; but for a while, beyond the fact that the London train was an hour or two behind its time, they could learn nothing. At last, through a by-stander, they gathered that there had been an accident on the line—he thought a collision, but was not sure, as it was next to impossible to get any precise details out of the railway staff. The two boys hung about, hearing ominous words now and then in disjointed scraps of conversation which increased their alarm.

"I can't stay here," said Jack at last; "let's go home."

They walked back in almost unbroken silence, for neither liked to betray to the other what was in his mind.

"Why didn't we ask a porter or somebody?" queried Brevoort. "We're not much the wiser for going now."

"They wouldn't have told us. They said the same thing to everybody—that the line was blocked, and that was all they knew themselves," answered

18

Jack, who had dreaded to ask lest he should have his fears confirmed by some terrible tidings.

"Well, likely we shall find the doctor back when we get in," said Heywood. "I only hope the old fellow we ran over won't turn up too, that's all!"

"Don't!" said Jack, uncomfortably.

"Don't what?"

"Talk as if it was sure to be all right."

They were at the school gates by this time, and went round to the back entrance.

"Brevoort," said Jack in a shaky whisper, "don't you think it would be better to get rid of that tricycle?"

"Not much!" said Brevoort. "Why on earth ——"

"Because it was given to me by that beastly Djinn of yours; and—and—I don't want to have anything more to do with it," answered Ainsley as he entered the school-room.

"Why, what do you mean? You don't think——"

"Yes, I do—and so do you. You *know* he's done this!"

"How do you make that out?" asked the American.

"You wished something would happen to stop the doctor from coming to-night; something *has*—

this collision—and—I call it beastly caddish of the Djinn," declared Jack, on the verge of tears.

Brevoort's sense of importance was ministered to by this suggestion, even though he was horrified, to do him justice, by the literal fidelity with which his wish had been granted.

"I guess it wasn't the Djinn's fault; he had to keep his promise, and he didn't see any other way just then. Mistakes will happen at first, and after all he'd only cause just enough collision to keep the doctor from coming to-night."

"How do you know? Suppose he never comes at all—not *alive.* O Heywood, it's awful! You don't know how jolly the poor doctor was—you've hardly seen him. And now perhaps he's—why couldn't you look out what you were saying?"

"I never meant it," said Brevoort sulkily. "I wasn't thinking of the wishes then. It's no use bullyragging me. And after all we don't *know* that the doctor's hurt at all."

"We know people do get hurt in collisions, and there's been one. Brevoort, don't look as if you didn't care. You would, if you knew what the doctor was. He took me to see the pantomime here the week before you came, and he was always trying to think of things to make the holidays less dull for us here—you know he was, yourself! What if he *was* strict now and then? I'd rather have a master like him than an easy-going duffer. And now he's hurt, killed perhaps—and it's all your fault and you stand there doing nothing."

"Why, blame it all, what am I to do?" demanded the American.

"You can do something; there's your other wish, use it and wish that the doctor isn't the least bit hurt; you must!"

The two boys stood opposite each other in the firelit school-room. Jack was desperately in earnest; he was a tender-hearted boy, and the idea that his head-master would never return alive drove him almost frantic. Many an act of consideration and kindness came back to him now; he reproached himself for all the mutinous and ungrateful expressions he had used. At bottom he had always liked the master; and he had spoken against the doctor only because the other fellows did and he didn't want to be thought a muff. And now he might never see the doctor's kind face again, might never hear the well-known voice commending him in work or games, unless Brevoort would act at once. And Brevoort stood there with exasperating coolness.

"If you don't," said Jack, "you'll be a murderer, and I'll tell everything."

"Hold on," returned Brevoort; "let's work out this thing a bit. I want to be dead sure of my facts. I'm anxious not to give myself away, don't you see? If the Djinn's gone and made such an ass of himself, will *any* wishing put it right? That's my difficulty."

"Oh, don't argue and jaw about it!" Jack burst out, impatiently. "*Try* it."

"Supposing there's been no collision, and the doctor's as well as anybody all this time, I shall have had my last wish and nothing to show for it."

"What does it matter, Brevoort? I'll never speak to you again if you don't wish."

"You talk as if it was so easy to make your mind up. Look what I might do with a wish like that! I could be the brightest, or the richest, or the strongest boy in the universe. I could wish to fly, if I chose! There's nothing I couldn't do—or be! And here you expect me to give up all that, and wish a perfectly ordinary wish, without ever know-ing how far there's any occasion for it."

"There *is* occasion! What fun would it be to be ever so rich or powerful and know that you might have saved the doctor if you liked and wouldn't?"

"Well," said Heywood reluctantly, "supposing I wish him safe back in town again—how'll that do?"

"No," said Jack. "You wished for something to stop him from coming back; and something always will, unless you prevent it. I want to be sure it's all right. Wish him back here safe and sound at once, then we shall know the Djinn hasn't muddled it this time."

"And supposing the doctor comes back now, and then that old chap calls, where shall we be then?" inquired Heywood.

"I don't care," replied Jack, "so long as nothing happens to the doctor. Nothing's as bad as that! Brevoort, you feel that as much as I do. You won't be such a brute as not to wish while there's still time! You can't!"

"There, then," said Heywood after a struggle; "I think it's all blamed foolishness, but sooner than hear you take on like that, here goes. I wish the doctor to come back safe and sound instantly!"

Both boys waited a little apprehensively, not quite sure whether their respected principal might not come bouncing in through the window, or down the chimney, or through the floor, propelled by the too literal Djinn, but nothing happened for two or three minutes.

"He's fetching him," said Heywood, under his breath.

"I hope he'll do it gently—without messing him about!" exclaimed Jack.

There came a ring at the bell, and a well-known voice was heard in the hall a moment or two later.

"The doctor!" shouted Jack, and broke down in hysterical laughter.

The doctor's voice was heard again, saying: "Walk in there, Kavanagh. I'll join you in a minute. You'll find a fire there."

And in walked Colonel Kavanagh.

"Ah," said the colonel when he saw the two boys, "and have you found your ring yet?"

"Not yet," answered Heywood.

"Then I suppose you haven't seen your Djinn again?"

"No," cried Jack, "and we don't want to see him! He's—he's a brute! That's what he is."

"What has the Djinn been up to now?" inquired Colonel Kavanagh.

"You won't tell anybody if we tell you?" Heywood asked.

"I can keep a secret, I think," answered the colonel. "You may trust me with it."

"Well," began Jack, "that Djinn has been— Oh,

you tell him, Brevoort! I hate to talk about it."

Colonel Kavanagh turned gravely to the American boy.

"Well," began Heywood, "we were riding that tricycle down hill, and it got a-going so that we couldn't stop it, and we ran into an old gentleman and he didn't like it——"

"I should not have liked it myself," commented the colonel as the American boy paused for breath.

"We told him we were sorry, and he said we were young ruffians; and then I sassed him, and he said he'd come and tell the doctor; and we didn't care, because we thought the doctor wouldn't be home till to-morrow——"

"But what has the Djinn to do with this?" asked the colonel.

"I'm coming to that," replied Heywood.

"You'll see soon enough," added Jack.

"Go on," said Colonel Kavanagh. "I'm all attention."

"Well," began Heywood again, "after we got back here we heard that the doctor would be home this afternoon, and we were afraid that the old boy would complain, because, you know, we oughtn't to have run into him, and I did sass him considerable."

"I fear that your conduct has been reprehensible," said the colonel, with a grave face, although there was a twinkle in his eye.

"And then—then I wished the doctor wouldn't come back this afternoon. And that was my second wish."

"Oh!" said Colonel Kavanagh. "And did the Djinn grant it?"

"Didn't he just!" cried Jack. "The beast!"

"The doctor didn't come when he was expected," Heywood went on, "and when we went to the station we heard that there had been an accident, and we knew that the Djinn had been up to mischief."

"I see," said the colonel; "you think that the Djinn caused the accident to carry out your wish that the doctor shouldn't come home?"

"That's just what he did," cried Jack.

"And what did you do?" asked Colonel Kavanagh.

"First off, we felt pretty mean about it; and then Jack begged me to use my third wish and bring the doctor back; and at last I did, and I hadn't wished it more'n three minutes before we heard his voice coming in the front door."

"Ah," said the colonel, "I think this is more extraordinary than your getting the tricycle; don't you?"

But before the boys could answer, the parlor-maid came in and said that the doctor was ready to receive Colonel Kavanagh in his study.

"You won't tell?" cried Jack, as the colonel was going.

"No," Colonel Kavanagh answered; "I will keep my promise. Your secret is safe."

The colonel's face was grave enough while he said this, but as he left the room a smile spread over his features. This smile still lingered when he entered the doctor's study, and the master of the school noticed it.

"What is the joke, Kavanagh?" he asked. "You were always fond of a laugh in the old days when we were school-boys together."

"But when we were school-boys together there never was a joke like this," answered Colonel Kavanagh. "And I can't tell you what this one is. I'm sworn to secrecy. You can tell me, something though. How is it that you are here now, although there has been a collision on the railway and the line is blocked?"

"That's simple enough," replied the doctor. "I came down by the other line, which takes one to Storchester, about ten miles from here on the coast. I had to see a man there on business. And I was walking over here when you met me and gave me a lift in your trap. It was rather cruel of me to accept your offer, too, since I took the only seat and forced your black servant to get down and walk in my stead."

"He won't mind the exercise," said the colonel; "he's a Sepoy, and he's used to long walks. I sent him here last night to ask if I might give the Ainsley boy—you know, I've known his mother a long time——"

"Yes. I know," assented the doctor.

"I sent to ask if I might give the boy a tricycle. I told his mother I'd look him up, and she let out that a tricycle was what he wanted. As you were not at home, I took the liberty of sending the man over again this morning with the tricycle."

"I allow tricycles," said the doctor.

"Then that's all right," the colonel went on. "Now, there's another favor I want to ask you. Don't tell the boy I sent him the tricycle."

"Doesn't he know?" asked the doctor.

"No."

"But where does he suppose it came from?" inquired the doctor. "He knows it doesn't rain tricycles."

"Perhaps he thinks it does—sometimes," said the colonel. "At all events, I want you not to inquire too curiously."

"As you please," the doctor answered.

"Then that is all settled satisfactorily," said Colonel Kavanagh, and he settled down to a cosey chat with his old friend the doctor.

Later in the evening, as the colonel was going away, he saw the tricycle in the hall, and he said to himself, "I wonder what will happen when that Yankee boy finds the ring?"

But nothing ever happened, for the ring was never found.

Pen and Ink.

Papers on subjects of more or less importance. By
BRANDER MATTHEWS. With a poem by Andrew
Lang and "An Epistle to the Author" in verse by
H. C. Bunner. Crown 8vo, half cloth, gilt top.

"There is a happy blending of wisdom and gaiety in these essays of Mr. Brander Matthews. While never profound they are seldom frivolous. Of sound common-sense there is plenty, and philosophy and moral instruction are not wanting. But when these occur they are sure to be whimsically stated, or to be standing shoulder to shoulder with some application or comment more or less fantastic."—ACADEMY.

"Mr. Matthews contrives to put into his essays a good deal of criticism and information, and if we do not agree with him at all points, it is partly because there are so many that there is room for difference of opinion here and there. His style is always clear, and if he is sometimes a little over-ingenious, as in his 'Philosophy of the Short Story,' he can plead in defence that this is the defect of his quality—that is, of a keen and discriminating intelligence."—NATION.

"Bright, suggestive, and thoughtful, they pleased many when they appeared, and will yield a more general pleasure now they are gathered into a book. Fugitive these critical disquisitions could scarcely be, collected or not. 'The True Theory of the Preface,' 'The Ethics of Plagiarism,' and the 'Philosophy of the Short Story,' treat of themes of permanent interest to bookmen and writers of fiction, and the treatment is decidedly individual and rousing. Mr. Matthews, as a critic and as a writer of short stories himself, is entitled to be heard on the subject of the 'Short Story,' and, both by definition and illustration, his discourse is notable."
—SATURDAY REVIEW.

"Mr. Brander Matthews not being a voluminous writer can afford to take time to be wise and witty. His 'Pen and Ink' papers may deservedly be classed under both of these heads."—LITERARY WORLD, Boston.

"The greatest charm to us of Mr. Matthews' writing is that air of restful, cultured ease that is apparent in all he does."—BUFFALO TIMES.

"Its brilliancy and humor, its polish and its general common sense, make it agreeable to the most jaded literary appetite."
— OVERLAND MONTHLY.

"On whatever subject he may select, Mr. Matthews is always cheerful, witty, and agreeable."—CHRISTIAN UNION.

"A better example of brilliant and recreative reading cannot be desired than we have in the bundle of varieties bound up in this well-made little volume."—INDEPENDENT.

"These essays exhibit a quality which is usually sought in the pages of Lamb and Montaigne. It is difficult to describe much more or to aptly denominate that quality."—AMERICAN HEBREW.

LONDON AND NEW YORK:

LONGMANS, GREEN, & CO.

POLITICAL AMERICANISMS.

A Glossary of Terms and Phrases Current at Different Periods in American Politics. By CHARLES LEDYARD NORTON. 16mo, ornamental cloth cover, $1.00.

LONGMANS, GREEN, & CO.,

15 East Sixteenth St., New York.

The Philosophy of Fiction in Literature

AN ESSAY

By DANIEL GREENLEAF THOMPSON, author of "A System of Psychology," "The Problem of Evil," "The Religious Sentiments of the Human Mind," etc. 12mo, $1.50.

"A most interesting work. It goes into the subject—does not skim over it."
—BOSTON POST.

"The author has contributed to the discussion of fiction in this volume in a very suggestive and valuable way. He covers the ground very fully in treating the sources, methods, and ends of fiction. His work is clear, comprehensive, sensible, and helpful."—PUBLIC OPINION.

"The author has sought to classify and describe the functions a work of fiction fulfills, the motives and materials with which it deals, and the principles by which its construction is governed. This task he has well performed; his method is free from pedantry, his attitude moderate and judicial."
—CRITIC (N. Y.)

"Mr. Thompson has written a work of supreme excellence, which cannot fail to be of value to every student of literature, no matter what his special vocation in that line may be. The book is one that will repay every young writer in its perusal and study. It is clearly reasoned and beautifully written."
—CHICAGO HERALD.

"No more important contribution to literary criticism has been made in recent years. . . It is clear cut, sensible (no mean praise) unprejudiced, sound."—THE DIAL (Chicago).

"The work done by Mr. Thompson can scarcely be too highly valued. He has discussed with absolute fairness and great ability certain important questions which have been recently haggled over with vehement declamation by the critics of fiction. He has brought to the elucidation of these questions all the clearness of vision and broad grasp of the subject which might be expected from the author of one of the foremost works on psychology of our time."
—BROOKLYN EAGLE.

"Mr. Thompson has expressed his thoughts with point and vigor. His criticisms of M. Zola's method . . are admirable and, it seems to us, unanswerable."—THE ACADEMY (Eng.).

"His discussion of the question (the relation of art to morals) is bold, sincere, liberal, and broad. We regret that we have not been able to call the attention of our readers earlier to this excellent book."—N. Y. INDEPENDENT.

LONGMANS, GREEN, & CO,

15 East 16th Street, New York.

www.ingramcontent.com/pod-product-compliance
Lightning Source LLC
Chambersburg PA
CBHW020846020726
47497CB00005B/1285